Blood
Remembered

Douglas Pratt

Blood Remembered is a work of fiction. Any names, places, characters, and incidents are products of the author's imagination or are used fictitiously. Any resemblance to actual persons, either living or dead, events, or locales is entirely coincidental.

Copyright © 2010 by Douglas Pratt

For Ashlee, thanks for pushing me
Princesss

1

The ringing of the phone pounded its way through the leaden slumber that held me tight to the bed. The taste of bourbon and cigars lingered around me like an over anxious car salesman. The phone finally ceased its incessant, wailing attempts to rouse me from the warm soft bed.

Unfortunately, the peace did not last long, as the ringing began again a second after it stopped. Since even seeing the back of my eyelids was barely possible, my eyes certainly couldn't focus on the digits illuminating from the clock. However, the internal clock inside my head was certain it hadn't reached the godlier hour of nine. Finally, annoyed and awake, I dragged myself through the early morning haze till my feet touched the soft carpet of the hotel room.

Waking in a hotel room often puts me into unusual sorts. The unanchored feeling comes from crossing back from the surreal world of the subconscious to an equally unfamiliar locale. For the first six or seven seconds, I am lost. I have to remember where I am, and in some cases who I am.

After a few seconds, my jagged memory pieced together the evening, and I remembered where I had fallen asleep. My present domicile was in a suite at the Royal Sonesta Hotel in New Orleans. It was a suite with a king-sized bed, a large bathroom with a Jacuzzi, and a mini bar. The sunlight was gleaming through the double French doors that lead out to a balcony. The wrought iron balcony hung four stories above Bourbon Street so one could sit and have an excellent panorama of the depravity that ravaged the street below.

I would have normally enjoyed the

large doors leading to the balcony, except that somehow some tremendously bright, retina-burning light was gleaming through the glass. I may have to talk to the management about this.

My hand fumbled around until it wrapped around the cell phone that was beginning to give me a minor seizure. Jerking it off the top of the table, I answered it before it could continue its horrendous wake-up call.

"Hello," my voice was hoarse and sounded groggy from a night of debauchery in the French Quarter.

"Max?" I immediately recognized the voice of Tom Campbell. Tom had been my father's lawyer, partner, and closest friend until my parents' death. Now he handles most of my legal affairs and my parent's estate from his office in my hometown of Hellenston. In the last ten years, he has managed to take my inheritance and double it in various investments. He makes the decisions and then briefs me, and all I do is sign my name and cash the checks. (Actually I think he cashes the checks, so I guess I am left to spend the money.) Of course, the situation works for him as he gets some very healthy percentages from these investments.

"Tom, what's up? Do you have any idea what time it is?"

"Yeah, Max, I've been up for over four hours, I actually have some information I thought you might be interested in."

"What?" My curiosity was picqued. Tom doesn't make it a habit of calling unless it is important. Certainly, anything I would be interested in at this hour had to be life and death.

"Amanda Rawls was arrested last night for murder."

The hangover that had threatened to ruin my day had suddenly vanished as a surge of adrenaline pumped through my body with hydraulic pressure. I don't know whether it was the mention of a murder or the association of Mandy's name with it.

"What? Who....who did she kill?"

"Mark Lofton."

"Her fiancé?"

"Ex-fiancé, he got married to another woman a week ago."

I had never met Mark; however, I had planned to go to the wedding that was scheduled for next month. I had not heard from Mandy in several months. I knew she was supposed to be getting married, and she had recently sent an invitation to the event.

"How long have he and Mandy been broken up?"

"I don't know yet. I am sure I will find out soon."

"Did she do it?" I was almost sure I knew the answer was no. However, a jilted lover is often capable of anything. But I have known Mandy for as long as I can remember.

Mandy and I met in high school. I was

in tenth grade and she had been a year behind me. We got to know each other one day when she and I had been paired together for a theater project. We performed a scene from *A Street Car Named Desire*. That spawned a relationship. We dated until the summer before my senior year, and we have always been close friends. She was my first love, and like most first loves, she was hard to forget.

After my parents' death, there was very little reason to stay in Hellenston, so I moved to Memphis. Mandy remained a good friend, and we continued to talk, just not as often. Like most people, our lives became more involved, and we let more time lapse between calls. Now we exchange an e-mail once in awhile.

"Well, she denies it," Tom said, " says she was out of town and came home to find him. But he was found in her living room, naked, with a hole in his chest. The .12 gauge was lying on the floor with her prints on it."

If Tom could defend her, there would be some assurance of her fate. Unfortunately, that wouldn't be the case. Last year, Tom was elected as the local prosecuting attorney. In a small town like Hellenston, often the prosecutors will still keep some of their clientele, like me. After all, there is only so much crime to prosecute. This could be bad news for Mandy, though. Besides being a genius with investments, Tom is a spectacular trial lawyer.

"Tom, does she have an attorney? I will pay the expenses if she can't"

"Max, I don't know about that. It might get costly."

I sighed, "Just let me know."

"You'll have to talk to her about that."

"Fine," I said looking at the Tag Heuer that was lying on the bedside table. The watch's hands indicated it was 7:46. "I'm in New Orleans right now, but I will be there tonight."

After a few minutes on the phone with Tom, I rang room service for some breakfast and something to quiet the gong reverberating inside my skull.

Standing in front of the mirror, I examined myself. The nicest thing one could say was that I was sporting a disheveled look. I rarely consider my physique overly attractive. I am not tall, only reaching the average height of 5'7 1/2". Unfortunately, I have a stocky build so I look a bit like a short wall. Luckily, the only real fat I have is a small paunch that likes to extend past my belt. I am pretty sure it is genetic because I have tried numerous exercises to get rid of it.

Bloodshot cobalt blue eyes stared into the mirror. The eyes exhibited the appearance of being fairly exhausted. Despite their current façade, women in my life have often remarked that the color of my eyes was quite sexy. However, the last lady who commented on me merely mentioned that the goatee I sometimes sported made me look like Satan. Of course, she did wait to declare this after we had broken off our relationship.

The stale aura that wafted off me from the long night beckoned me to shower. A hot shower would help my mind work since the adrenaline rush that had cured my hangover awhile ago had vanished leaving me with a brick inside my head. Still, I had to gather my thoughts.

I recalled the last time I had seen Mandy. It had been almost four years ago, maybe longer. She had come to Memphis for a weekend. I couldn't even remember why she had been there. After a delicious dinner at Automatic Slims, I took her down to Beale Street to hear some blues. After several rounds, we were dancing and having a good time. Despite some heavy kissing, she had gone back home the next day without any consequences. There was some talk about getting together again to see where things might lead, but nothing serious ever came about. Then she met Mark Lofton a month or so later. He was a forklift driver or something at Wal-Mart. I fell into a couple of other beds, and she never came back to Memphis. I hadn't really thought about it till now, but I now wondered, "What if?"

The steaming water coursed over me. My hair had been lathered with the complimentary shampoo provided by the hotel, and the soap mingled with the water as it flowed down the drain. With my hair full of suds, I found my razor. I needed to keep the stubble around my beard trimmed. I hated shaving cream, but I could never get a close enough shave with an electric razor. I started using a nice, simple razor in the shower.

Once out of the shower, I was on the phone to Nicole Powell. Nikki is, for lack of a better term, my secretary. She is in Memphis. Basically, she takes care of all my little details for a slight compensation. Not that her salary supports her. She is working her way through law school at the University of Memphis. Most of her time is spent studying. When her nose is not buried in a book, she does little things for me. She pays my bills, or forwards them to me. She takes any phone calls for me and relays the messages to me. She is the only person who knows exactly where I am at any point and time. I simply pay her about $300 a week to keep me organized.

Besides, there is a powerful cliché that behind every great man there is a woman keeping him straight. Now I may not be great, but she surely keeps me in line.

"Nikki, did I wake you?" I said into the phone.

"No, honey, I am always up waiting on your calls." Her sarcastic and witty sense of humor has always appealed to me. She is a very attractive lady only a few years my junior. Her father, James Powell, was a professor that taught my History of Journalism class at U of M. He became something of a mentor to me. He invited me over several times for dinner, and he got me an internship at The Memphis Daily. A bond developed between me and his family. Sadly, he left his wife a few years back for a young student. They vanished to parts unknown. Nikki was the same age as the student that ran away with Dr. Powell. She never talks about it, but I could sense some disgust and possibly disdain.

"I am sorry to bother you, but I need to go to Hellenston."

"Problem?" We are both sympathetic to our respective pasts.

"Small one, but not mine."

"Are you going to share it with me?"

"Well, I am in a bit of a hurry. Could you find me a room?" I had already begun packing my clothes into my backpack. "Or maybe someplace secluded? Like a cabin."

"Sure, when are you going to be there."

"I'll probably leave here after lunch. It'll take most of the day. I should be there by tonight"

"You got it; I'll call you back in a few minutes."

She hung up before I had much of a chance to agree with her.

A knock on the door indicated my breakfast had arrived, so I opened the door to a room service attendant, an African-American girl in her mid twenties, in with my small feast, an omelet with onions, red peppers, ham and cheese, coffee, a pint of orange juice, and a bottle of Advil. She presented me with the bill that explained to me that I spend way too little for eggs and ibuprofen at the store. I signed it to my room. I grabbed my wallet and gave the girl, whose name was also Nicole, a ten dollar bill. I was familiar with the way service charges worked. Out of the 17% service charge that the hotel tacked onto my $37 breakfast, Nicole would only see about

$1.50, maybe $2.00. The rest was divided among the other room service attendants.

There have been accusations of my generosity being too pretentious. However, the peons in life are important, and they always remember the tippers. It was a truth I learned in Florida one Christmas. There was a doctor who came down only once a year to play some golf and snorkel. He believed in tipping everyone well, and the service he received amazed me. From the minute he walked into the hotel, everyone from the bellhop to the hotel manager treated him like royalty. Even though he was a doctor, he was no billionaire even though he was treated like he was. Since then I decided that he had the right idea, a little green entices everybody.

After breakfast, I decided to pack my gear before I step down the hall to Patrick's room to tell him I was leaving. Patrick Labatt and Cynthia Williams were my drinking mates this weekend. Patrick and I

met at the University of Memphis. We
became fast friends, good drinking buddies,
and lifetime compadres. He and his
girlfriend, Cynthia, moved to New Orleans
last year to obtain his doctorate in literature.
Yesterday was Patrick's birthday, and I had
come to New Orleans to celebrate. Since we
had intended to do some intense partying, I
got a suite at the Royal Sonesta so we
wouldn't have to stumble too far. We had
certainly invested some of my retirement
funds in almost every bar along the French
Quarter. We were pretty snockered by the
time we stumbled to our rooms early this
morning.

If they felt anything like I did, they
were not going to appreciate the early
morning wakening. I finished packed my
belongings. I thought I was moving quickly,
but in retrospect, I think the room was the
one moving quickly. I just tried to hang on
to the bed so I wasn't thrown from the hotel.

I finally finished filling my suitcase. I

glanced at my watch. It was only 8:30. I decided I needed to pop next door to let Patrick and Cynthia know that I had to leave. I didn't know if I would be able to wait until after lunch to leave.

I knocked for several minutes before I heard the stirring on the other side of the door.

Cynthia's face appeared in the crack of the door. "Max, what are you doing up?"

She looked fairly hung over; an effect that was caused by all the Hurricanes and Mango Daiquiris that she had imbibed.

"I have an emergency. I have to leave soon."

A worried look passed over her face, "What's wrong honey?"

"An old friend of mine is in trouble. I have to go home."

Patrick stumbled up behind her and opened the door wider. At this point, I could make out that they were both naked. Cynthia had covered herself with a sheet, but it left little to the imagination. Patrick didn't bother covering himself for me.

"What's wrong, Max? You have to go back to Memphis?"

"No, Hellenston."

"What's wrong?" Cynthia chimed.

"One of my old friends has a little legal problem. The police seem to have found her fiancé on her living room floor with a hole in his chest. She was standing beside him with a .12 gauge shotgun lying on the floor."

Cynthia's eyes widened, "She killed him?"

"I don't know yet. But she may need a lawyer. I am going to see if she needs anything. She may need some financial help. I just want to make sure everything is okay with her."

Patrick's eyes narrowed a little, "Well, do you need any help?"

"No," I answered, "you have school next week, don't you?"

Patrick nodded. I was sure that Patrick

would have loved to join me.

"Are you staying in Hellenston?" he asked, and I could sense the underlying thoughts.

"I guess so. Nikki is working on getting me a place."

"Who is it?" Cynthia asked.

"Mandy Rawls. She was an old high school girlfriend."

I could see Patrick nodding with a familiar look.

"Don't worry about the hotel; the bill is already taken care of. Just enjoy the rest of your stay. And happy birthday."

"Thanks, man," he said, "but if you need anything, call me."

"Don't worry."

I gave Cynthia a quick kiss on the cheek and told them that I would see them soon. Patrick gave me a quick embrace and warned me to be careful. I assured him that I was always careful. He knew me well enough to know that I was never careful.

2

After I left Patrick and Cynthia's room, I returned to my room. I picked up my bag and left a few dollars for the maid. I checked the room to make certain I had not left anything before I shut the door. The elevator opened to the bright lobby. The Royal Sonesta had a beautiful lobby that was decorated in sunny colors and filled with fresh, colorful flowers. I walked from the elevator to the front desk. A large crystal chandelier hung from the ceiling

I checked out of my room with a tall man who offered to have the valet bring my car around while I reviewed the itemized bill. I gave him my credit card, and I paid for the rest of Patrick and Cynthia's stay. I had the clerk, whose name was Simon, take care of dinner for Patrick and Cynthia in the restaurant.

It was still early, and valet traffic was slow. The valet arrived just a moment after I had walked out the entrance. He pulled up with my 1998 BMW Z3, and I expressed my gratefulness to him with a picture of Andrew Jackson to remember me.

I drove out of New Orleans along Interstate 10 toward Baton Rouge. Once I had gotten out of the city, I called Tom to let him know what I was doing. He was not in his office, but I left a message with his secretary, Mrs. McEwan. Mrs. McEwan is a wonderfully, crotchety old hag. Everyone has known one of those people who has made a life out of being miserable, and that person is only happy when they are nearing death. Well, Mrs. McEwan is the mother of that person and the cause of his tribulation. She is the widow of an elder of the Church of Christ, and she feels it is her duty to rain on everybody's parade. She began working for Tom and my father when I was a tiny thing. She has always been very good at her job, but she has always been an overbearing, rigid woman. I always dreaded her company. As anyone could tell, I love her as dearly as one loves a festering boil, and I think she reciprocates those feelings for me (and probably everybody else.) She loves to point out my lack of regular employment, and she regards me as blight.

"Mrs. McEwan, this is Max Sawyer. Is Tom in the office?"

"Mr. Campbell is meeting with Judge Hurt." Her other pet peeve is the fact that I use Tom's first name, despite the fact that he could be my father. She has the ideology that all young people are whipper-snappers and should know their place. Of course, her idea of a young person is someone not over 45.

"Please inform him that I will be in Hellenston late this evening."

"Must be nice. I certainly wish I could

take any little jaunt that I wanted to, but I am certainly tied down by my work."

"Now, Mrs. McEwan, you know I keep banker's hours. I was up early this morning before I realized I had nothing to do."

"Yes, Mr. Sawyer."

That was the extent of most of our conversations. It always seems that she practices the three Bees of communication; she berates, belittles, and begrudges. I suppose that if it weren't for the fact that she hates everyone but herself and Jesus, I might be offended. I only hope for her sake that Jesus remains on her good side.

I hung up with her. I set the cruise control at 67 miles per hour. Even though I could make excellent time in this car, I try not to speed. This car looks like its doing sixty when the keys are in my pocket.

I fiddled in the ashtray for the remote to the CD changer. I clicked it a few times until I found B.B. King belting out one of my favorites, "Ain't That Just Like a Woman."

With his deep voice extolling the virtues of womankind, I drove north toward home and a handful of unexpected surprises.

3

There are times when one starts to do something, or when one anticipates something that a sick feeling climbs into their skin. This feeling stretches beyond the physical and mental and envelops the whole essence of a person. Psychics have noted that prior to certain catastrophic events that they have similar feelings that leave them nauseated, exhausted, and in some cases comatose.

I don't necessarily give much credence to what psychics say that they experience; however, I felt a foreboding that knotted my stomach and made me quite foggy as I drove north toward my hometown. Of course, it may have been the countless bourbon and Cokes that I had imbibed the night before. I had not been back in over two years, so right at the moment, I was beginning to consider turning back around and returning to New Orleans to try to rid myself of the horrendous hangover that had returned to haunt me. Upon later reflection, that would have been the better of the two choices.

The few times that I have returned to Hellenston, Arkansas have been quick trips. I hadn't spent a night in the town in over a decade. The last night I spent in the town was the night before my high school graduation, almost two weeks after I found my parents murdered in their bed. Within one month, I found their murderer, Sheriff Frank Hanson. Hanson had been a corrupt cop, and my father had discovered a slew of illegal activities that his department had perpetrated. Hanson entered our home late one night and shot both of my parents in their sleep. I had been out late with Beth Ann Warren. I had sneaked into the house to avoid the wrath of my father. I found them the next morning.

Hanson had been careless. He thought he could control the murder investigation. I found some of the evidence that my father had on Hanson. Hanson had been so cocky that he never suspected a high school kid could connect him. I walked away from this town the day after he and three of his deputies had been sentenced to prison terms. Hanson was given the death penalty, but ten years later he is still rotting away on death row.

Suddenly I found myself an 18-year-old, orphaned multimillionaire. That didn't leave me without any family, unfortunately. My dad's family lived for the most part in Atlanta. My grandfather was a retired Baptist pastor. He used to work hard to save me from eternal damnation after my parents' death. He was never keen on the fact that my father had switched teams to the church of Christ when he married my mother. He always tried to mention it in the least subtle way possible, usually in some way to irritate my mother. I rarely visit them, and they have never come to me.

Things got hairy after my parents' death. I think there were some sore feelings from my aunt and uncle that my father didn't leave any of his wealth to them. Or perhaps because Tom had been named his executor instead of one of them. My grandparents attempted to guilt me into moving to Atlanta to be close to family.

Not that I don't appreciate them, but they march to a different drummer than I do. Granddad always feels the need to subject everyone to his moral standard, and if they don't walk his line then they must be wrong. There is very little elbow room to maneuver in his world.

My grandmother was never that demanding. She was a good grandmother who believed she was only placed upon this earth by God for the sole purpose of spoiling her grandkids. I don't know exactly what she did before she had grandkids, but I am sure she was nowhere near as much fun. I, unfortunately, was not the first grandchild nor was I a favorite. That lucky duty fell on Michelle, my oldest cousin. Her mother was my father's older sister.

Luckily, they couldn't get to me, and I moved to Memphis, Tennessee where I attained a degree in journalism. I worked for a year at The Memphis Daily, the local newspaper. I retired early after a disagreement with my editor, who would probably say that I had gotten myself fired. I decided to go back to school, and for a few years, I became a professional student eventually getting degrees in English, film, and business. To quote the Dire Straits' song, now, with the help of Tom Campbell and several investment specialists, "I get money for nothing and my chicks for free." This has lead to a life of travel and an interesting career in debauchery.

Now I was about to return to my roots

and not without a fair share of in trepidation. I had this almost unspeakable dread as I drove through Louisiana and Arkansas. Despite my ill feelings about returning, the route north took me through some of the most beautiful scenery. As I watched the numerous fields of green, it became easy to forget I was en route to a murder. So I enjoyed the breeze through my hair and the sound of Eric Clapton tributing Robert Johnson.

Twelve hours, 637 miles, and five bathroom breaks later, I found myself approaching the all too familiar outskirts of Hellenston.

Even though I have been back a few times in the past ten years, it still amazed me how the town had made some changes. Little shopping centers are built every couple of years, most of them only house one or two stores, but the new buildings still throw me for a loop.

Hellenston had a quaint town square.

Several years before I left for college, the town was in shambles. Nothing was being cared for. The courthouse looked old and run down, and the shops were dingy. Fortunately, the previous mayor was voted out of office.

Since then, the town cleaned itself up with a Help Heal Hellenston Campaign. The mayor and city council formed a committee to beg, borrow, and accept grant money for the advancement of the city. The committee formed sub-committees to tackle different areas of the town.

The sub-committees, no doubt, formed sub-sub-committees, which may or may not have formed sub-sub-sub-committees. Whatever they did, it worked wonders. Now the square was beautiful, like a scene from Norman Rockwell. The courthouse gleams white again, and the stores look less like vacant spaces and more like shops. Hellenston has become a tourist stopover with its charming antique shops, an old-fashioned soda fountain, and a legion of local events, like the Riverfest that was happening this weekend.

Riverfest was an annual event that has happened every September since before I could remember. It involved a plethora of activities from a crafts fair, a homemade sailboat race, a crawfish eating contest (called the Mud Lobster Jamboree with a live bluegrass band,) and a small fair. When I say it is a small fair, I mean it has one Ferris wheel and at least one other contraption that would fling one around until the funnel cakes spewed forth. Don't get me wrong, I loved this weekend when I was a kid. I would spend all Saturday at the fair with my friends. We ate so much junk food that we would be too sick to make it to church on Sunday. Not that my mother ever thought that such an excuse would fly.

I drove along Main Street. It was a nine o'clock on a Thursday night. The streets had a few kids cruising along. I chuckled when I passed a "No Cruising" sign. Cruising was all a high school kid could do on a Saturday night in a town like Hellenston. There had only been one movie theater in town, and the movie was almost always two or three weeks late getting to us. There was only so much that small town kids can do. Hang out at the Dairy Queen and then drive across town to see who was hanging out at Sonic. Poor kids now had to get by with just drugs and sex. That is probably the downfall of our society right there. Old people who don't want to see kids. Out of sight, out of mind. It is a shame, I thought. Probably one of the solutions found by the sub-committee in charge of hiding the children.

As I drove past the town, I saw the empty building that had once been the Dairy Queen. I guess without the kids, the Queen had no one to support her. What kind of town doesn't have a Dairy Queen?

I thought back to the days of my youth. When I was still carefree, I could still see the group of cars parked in the parking lot of the Price Chopper grocery store. I had spent many hours on the weekend here. I imagined life when the only thing that mattered was what time I had to be home. I was suddenly sinking into a pit. I sat thinking about my childhood. Those are the things often taken for granted.

I pushed the thoughts out. It was time to focus on the present. I had called Nikki when I passed through Little Rock. She had rented a large houseboat on the river. Since it was so late, the marina owner had agreed to leave the keys in an envelope taped to the door. I drove north on Highway 16 to Pryor's Bay Marina. The marina was off the highway down a small paved road astutely named Pryor's Bay Marina Drive. The little road wound through some wooded hills for a mile and a half before it ended at the parking lot of the marina.

I was looking forward to being on the water again. I am pretty sure I was born underwater. I have always shared an affinity to boats and water with my father. We often took his boat up and down the river, or we vacationed near the ocean where we would sail out to sea for a few days before ever returning to shore.

I have continued my love for the water ever since. I am always excited when I get to spend some time on a boat. The boat was fabulous. It was christened the Elizabeth Ann II, and it slept, 14 people. Actually, it could only sleep 14 if one were into the orgy style of 7 people per bed. The Elizabeth Ann also sported a hot tub, a full kitchen, digital satellite, GPS system, and, probably most importantly, a full bar with three different brands of bourbon: Makers Mark, Old Charter, and Knob Creek.

I poured a short shot of the Knob Creek and gingerly put it to my lips where I instantly devoured it. I settled in quickly and found my berth. I have always loved sleeping on the water, and within minutes, I was sleeping like a baby. A baby that had been nursing a giant hangover for over 600 miles.

4

I hate alarm clocks. There is something downright evil about disrupting anything as peaceful as a good night's sleep. Besides, I have always known two things: one, there is nothing that happens before 9 a.m. that is so important that it won't wait until 10, and two, I let my body rest until it doesn't need any more, because tomorrow night I may not get any sleep.

So at the crack of eleven I awoke. I sat up on the bed, and I adjusted to my surroundings. The sunlight was squeezing through the blinds. I stretched and turned in the bed. I felt rejuvenated. On the table beside the bed were three books that I had picked up in New Orleans. One of my favorite things to do is read. I am always in the middle of a book of some sort. Being a bibliophile of epic proportions, I have quite a collection that ranges from rare and vintage books to new, modern fiction. I picked up one of the books, the first edition of Dashiell Hammett's *The Thin Man*. I thumbed to the first chapter and quickly read for a few minutes before I climbed out of bed.

After a quick shower, I dressed. My pocket supplies were on the bedside table. They consisted of anything I might need in an emergency: a cell phone, a pocket knife, a small black Mag-Lite, a gold Zippo, I had given up smoking except for the occasional cigar, but the lighter was my bad habit, and a wine tool, in case I run into an exceptionally dangerous bottle of Pinot Grigio. I loaded my pockets with my cache of gadgets.

I found that the refrigerator was freshly loaded with milk, juice, and Bud Light. I wondered if the marina always stocked these boats before renting them, or if Nikki had made the arrangements. Either way, I was grateful as I found a box of Rice Krispies.

After my breakfast, I walked off the boat. I wanted to see Tom and let him know I had arrived.

Tom's office is located down from the courthouse on Main Street. I parked in a metered space and proceeded down to his office. Tom is probably one of the most prosperous attorneys in the whole area. A lot has to do with the commission he makes off of my estate as well as the money that he and my father made together, but he is also one of the best litigators I have ever known. And with the exception of my father, he is the most honest lawyer I have ever known. Hellenston now had a fine prosecutor. While the murder was on the docket at the moment, Tom would most likely get his share of less heinous criminals to lock up. I'm sure he would see his fair share of drunks and penny ante drug dealers.

When I entered the office, the little bell tinkled, and Mrs. McEwan looked up from her crossword puzzle. She has been an avid crossword puzzle fan since they were first invented.

"He isn't here, Mr. Sawyer. He is in court." She nodded toward the courthouse and then turned back to her puzzle as if I had already left.

"Thanks," I replied. She didn't move except to continue filling in her little boxes. I quickly turned and left.

I strolled down the sidewalk. Being home always made me feel weird. It was hard to pinpoint exactly. There were so many memories I had here, and then there were so many that I tried to forget. Yet, I felt so peaceful when I walked down these familiar streets. The faces of the people around were nice. No one seemed capable of frowning today. There is something comforting about living in a small town that often people take for granted. Big cities, like

Memphis, tend to have sterilized citizens. Everyone is afraid to look at each other for fear that they may become involved in some sort of interaction. I can only imagine what even larger cities were like. That comfort level in a small town gives everyone a sense of security.

I reached the courthouse and climbed these very familiar steps. Inside it wasn't hard to find the courtroom, considering there is only one. I had been inside the courtroom many times as a child. I would either watch my father making motions or defending someone who had gotten drunk and pissed on the manger scene in front of the Hellenston Methodist Church. I remember my father making jokes with Tom about the guy after he was fined $500 for vandalism and an indecent exposure. Dad had said that he could have gotten him off if he hadn't decided to do it during the church's reenactment of the first Christmas. Dad had joked that it might have changed the whole meaning of Christmas.

I spoke with one of the bailiffs who told me that court would be recessed in about twenty minutes for lunch. I decided I could wait twenty minutes, and I found a bench. I reached into my pocket and removed my Zippo. It was truly a bad habit of mine. I always find myself playing with it. Usually snapping it open and shut. Occasionally I enjoy flipping it with one hand and catching it with the other. If I get really bored I have been known to try to flip it while it is lit.

I remained seated until the doors opened and the lawyers were filing out of the courtroom. Tom was carrying his papers together as he came through the door.

"Tom."

Tom turned slowly till I saw his jolly round face. His gray beard and round body often left him playing Santa Claus at holiday parties.

"Max!" His voice was excited. While

we talked at least twice a week,

I hadn't seen Tom since he and Cathy came to Memphis last year. I shook his hand firmly. I cannot help smiling when I look into his jovial face.

"So, what's the word?" I asked.

"Well, I can't tell you much. The evidence against her does look very good for this. She does have an attorney, for now, at least."

"No problem, who is he?"

"Charlie Nichols, he is a good attorney," Tom lifted his briefcase from the table. "I don't think she will be able to afford him if it goes to trial."

"Well, I will have a talk with him. What about bail?"

Tom released a small sigh, "There has been no indictment yet, so no bail has been set. I probably won't push hard to deny bail. I don't think she will go anywhere. I know you and she has been friends, but I will be honest with you, it looks bad for her. There are some extenuating circumstances, though."

"Tom, I still want to talk to her. I will wait and see about the bail, but she may need some help."

Tom nodded in agreement, "Well, want to grab a bite to eat? I bet you have been running since I called you yesterday."

"Yeah, you interrupted a perfectly good hangover. But, I ate a late breakfast. Let me have a talk with Charlie Nichols and Mandy first. Maybe dinner?"

"That sounds fine. Come by the house and Cathy can fix a nice dinner."

"How is Cathy?"

"She's great," Tom began, "I told her you were coming. She can't wait to see you. Where are you staying?"

"I rented a houseboat over at Pryor's Bay."

"Those are expensive. Why not stay out at the house or with us?"

"I didn't know if I would be taking up

too much space. Besides, I thought you had rented the house?"

"It was. They moved out a few weeks ago. Still, you can stay at the house. Save some money."

"I don't think I could stay there. Besides, you know what I think. Money is just something you need to kill the time until you die."

"Yes, I can tell."

I smiled.

Tom pointed the way toward Charlie Nichols office. Ten minutes later, I found him alone in his office reviewing paperwork. His office was a bit barren compared to Tom's. He had no secretary, and his office was filled with old furniture that looked like he had purchased at a flea market. I wasn't encouraged.

"Mr. Nichols," I said as I entered the door to his office.

"Yes, may I help you?" he straightened up at his desk.

"I want to speak with you about Amanda Rawls."

"Yes, what can I do for you?" His voice had an air of suspicion in it.

"My name is Max Sawyer," I extended my hand to shake his.

"Max Sawyer?" His mind flipped through his memory like a Rolodex.

"Aren't you Ronald Sawyer's son?"

"Yes, I am."

"I was terribly sorry about his death. He was a good lawyer and a good man. It was awful. I am very glad that those two got the..." He paused, apparently aware of my discomfort.

"Thank you," I muttered. Then I diverted the subject, "Mandy Rawls is a close friend of mine. I wanted to talk to you if I could about her."

"I can't talk to you about a case, sorry."

"Can she afford to pay you?"

He simply answered, "I don't know. I can't tell you anything without her permission."

"Fair enough. I understand. I would like to talk to her. If she is in financial straits, then I would like to pay you to defend her. Is that possible?"

"That would depend on her," he suddenly realized he would make more than he had planned with this case.

I had sat down opposite his desk, "Can I get in to see her?"

"I'll call the sheriff office. It shouldn't be a problem, though."

"Thanks, can you share some of the details? You know, just the stuff that I could find out with a little research. Save me some time."

"Well," Nichols began, "she was found by the deputies shortly after the shooting in the house with the victim, Lofton, who was naked. The shotgun was found on the floor with her prints on it. The state police sent their crime lab to investigate. The shells didn't have any prints on them at all. Ms.

49

Rawls didn't have any powder burns on her either."

"Who called the police?"

"It was a call to the receptionist desk reporting a shot being heard. The sheriff responded and found her, basically over the body. She said that she had just gotten in from Little Rock and found him that way."

I leaned back in my chair. The case did sound weak for Mandy. "Now, I understand that Lofton had just broken off his engagement with Mandy and married someone else, correct?"

Nichols nodded slowly and reached into his drawer and retrieved a pack of Dunhill cigarettes. He offered one to me, and while I would prefer a Dunhill cigar, I politely accepted one from his pack.

"So, who is the grieving widow?" I asked as he handed his lighter to me. I lit my cigarette with the lighter, which was a fancy one with a blue flame.

"Leigh Rozen, she owns Herbs and

More outside of town."

I handed his lighter across the desk, "I love your lighter. I have a friend with one. Those aren't cheap either."

"It was a Christmas gift," he said as he slid the shining silver lighter into his vest pocket.

"Listen," I said as I leaned forward, "I want to speak with Mandy today. Can you go ahead and arrange it?"

"No problem, just give me a minute, and I'll call the sheriff's office to let them know you are on your way."

"Thanks." I rose from my seat and shook his hand, "I will head that direction then."

He nodded to me as I turned to go, "I will be talking to her in a little while. She will have to let me know that I can talk to you about her case."

"She will," I said very matter-of-factly.

Nichols smiled, "That's fine."

I returned his smile and turned to leave.

I stopped and picked up one of his business cards, "In case I need to call you."

"Wait," he said, "I have a new number." He dug into a white box and pulled out another card. "Here are my new cards."

The cards looked identical, but I slid them into my pocket and turned to walk out the door.

5

The sheriff's office is in the building behind the courthouse. It was only a few minutes walk back toward the courthouse. I stopped by my car to feed the meter. The last thing I needed was a ticket from these cops.

My little stroll took me down Main Street. I walked along the street and enjoyed the beautiful afternoon. I walked along the sidewalks that looked as if they were only a few years old. Perhaps that too had been a project of the Help Heal Hellenston Campaign. It seemed to have given the town a fresh look compared to my recollection of the grungy look Main Street had once had.

The sheriff's office looked like it was in the process of renovation itself. The building was encased in scaffolding, and it was being attended to by numerous men painting and repairing its exterior. The inside of the office had obviously not been budgeting for renovation this year and reminded me of a makeshift trailer office with wood paneling covering every wall, and the ceiling marked with the fake tile that gives the appearance that it was textured.

The receptionist's counter was to the right of the door. Behind the counter was an older woman who would have given Mrs. McEwan a run for her money at church. She sat reading a thick Bible. Bifocals hung on the tip of her nose. On the counter sat a cross-stitched cross that looked a bit askew in its frame.

When the door shut and I stepped in front of the counter, she peered over the wire rims at me like Mrs Stewart, my third-grade teacher, had done after I was caught practicing my kissing on Angie Tenom, the most beautiful blond haired girl in the fourth grade. It was a good kiss, but it had nothing on the one I gave her behind the scoreboard during the Homecoming game in ninth grade. I paused for a moment and wondered if Angie still lived in town. It might be a worthwhile effort to look her up.

"May I help you?" Her breath poured out of her mouth filled with the aroma of cigarettes and mints and interrupted my notion. I noticed that she didn't have an ashtray on her desk.

"Yes, ma'am. I am here to see Amanda Rawls."

"Are you Mr. Sawyer?" she asked.

"Yes, ma'am. Mr. Nichols was supposed to have called."

"Please have a seat. It will be a few minutes." I glanced at my watch. It read 1:17.

I sat down and picked through the magazines lying in the reception area. I finally stumbled across a travel magazine called *Southern Harmony*. So I began to flip through it. There was a great article on Mountain View, a town not far from Hellenston. Mountain View was featured as a great getaway for weekenders. The magazine had some great pictures of the town, featuring some of the locals pickin' and a grinnin'. Mountain View was known for a few things. It had been bestowed the title of Folk Music Capital of the World. Whether the town's nickname was self-bestowed, I didn't know. It was also the hometown of the actor Dick Powell who starred in over 50 movies. My personal favorite had been *Murder, My Sweet* where he played the hard-boiled detective, Philip Marlowe. Now he was no Humphrey Bogart, but he didn't have Lauren Bacall as a leading lady.

At ten till two, the receptionist stood up, "If you will follow Deputy Sanders." Her hand rose slowly and she pointed her bony finger as if she was the Ghost of Christmas Past.

I followed the deputy down a corridor and into a room.

"I'll have to frisk you," he replied.

"Okay," I turned my back toward him, "just make sure I get my money's worth."

He grunted as his hands patted me up and down.

"Okay, have a seat."

I obeyed and sat at a large wooden table. The room was empty except for the table and chairs. The floor was covered in a pale yellow tile that was designed in the seventies and sprinkled with grated cheese, and I got the impression that this was probably used more as a lunch room than an interrogation room.

Ten minutes passed before the door opened, and Mandy was escorted in the room. Her eyes lit up the moment she saw me.

"Max, what are you doing here?" Her voice sounded as tired as her eyes looked.

"Came to visit you." The deputy shut

the door, but I figured he was just on the other side. "Looks like I caught you at a bad time?"

She slumped in the chair, "Yeah, what are you doing here?"

"I heard you were in trouble. I came to see what I could do."

"Oh Max, they are going to...I don't know what they are going to do."

I sat in the chair next to hers and touched her hand. I could feel the fear trembling its way through her body.

"Tell me about it, Mandy."

"I didn't do it. I really didn't"

"I believe you. But it doesn't look good. Let me ask you this once, and only once, okay?"

She nodded slowly

"Did you kill Mark Lofton?" I asked and then added, "Maybe in self-defense?"

"No, I said I didn't do it. I came home and found him that way."

"Where were you that night then?" I

touched her hand again and held it for a second.

"I had gone to Little Rock to visit Austin." Austin had been a mutual friend of ours in high school. I had not seen him since I left Hellenston.

"How long were you there?"

"Several hours, I left here about six and got back about two in the morning."

"You were with Austin the entire time?"

"Yes," she said in a hoarse whisper, "we got together every so often. Have dinner. Catch a movie. That night we had pizza and watched *The Princess Bride*."

I smiled slightly; it had been her favorite movie. I let go of her hand and leaned back in my chair. "When did you and Mark break the engagement?" I didn't know a nicer way of asking, but now was not the time to worry about being nice.

"He did it about two weeks ago. Then he got married to that...that..."

"Leigh Rozen?"

"Yeah, she's a crack whore." Mandy's mouth frothed with bitterness like a rabid animal.

"User or a dealer?"

"Both I would bet. I know she is a dealer. Most people are getting their stuff from her."

"She hasn't lived here long?"

"Few years now."

"When was the last time you saw Mark?" I leaned forward again. I couldn't help noticing how tired she looked, but she still had that simple charm that she always did.

"A couple of days ago. I guess it was Wednesday night. The day before the...before he..."

I grabbed her hand, "Where did you see him?"

"Food Plus. He tried to talk to me. I was crying and screaming at him that I wanted him to leave me alone."

"Have the two of you been together at all since the breakup?"

"Just that time."

"Mandy, was he trying to start something with you? Did he want to continue seeing you?"

"I...I don't know. He just kept saying that he wanted a minute to explain, but I walked out."

I had to admit that the more Mandy talked the worse it made her case sound. Or maybe the better. I could never imagine that the sweet girl who had been my first love could do that. Self-defense made sense. If he wanted to continue their relationship in spite of his new bride, then her rejection might spurn an attack by him. An attempted rape, perhaps.

"It is going to be all right. We are going to figure this out."

She stretched her arms out and wrapped them around my neck. I held her for several minutes as she buried her face against my shoulder. I think she felt relief that she was not going to be alone in this.

"Can you afford your attorney?" I asked her.

"Not really," she stated.

"Okay, I am going to pay for him. He said he would be by later to talk to you. If you want my help, then let him know. Okay?"

She nodded with a tear in her eye.

6

I walked out of the sheriff's office after spending half an hour with Mandy. As soon as she was escorted back, I was on the phone to Tom. I left the sheriff's office and walked through the dark October evening as I talked to him.

"I will post the bail. I want her out of jail today, Tom."

"There is no way that she will get out today. She may have to stay all weekend. She may not have a bail hearing until Monday or Tuesday. Besides, all I can do for you in that respect is assure you the money is there. Remember I am the prosecution, whether I like it or not. I don't want to be disbarred."

"Fine, then I will call Nichols and have

him arrange it." I was almost to my car.

"That will work better. Are you going to come out for dinner?" Tom asked.

"As soon as I call Nichols."

"Well, if you are hungry for some delicious lasagna, be there tonight about seven."

"I am already starving."

I called Nichols and told him what I wanted. His comments were about the same as Tom's. Mandy may not get out until Monday.

I slid my phone back into my jacket pocket. The autumn air felt great as I inhaled long deep breaths of the pure Ozark air.

Voices up the road were approaching. I walked along quietly thinking about Mandy and Mark.

"Max Sawyer?" I jerked my head toward the voice. "Is that you, Max?"

The sun struck me in the eyes. I could only make out a female. "Yes?" I answered.

"It's Lisa. Lisa Day." The figure got

closer, and I recognized another old girlfriend. Although in all honesty Lisa and I never got to be that hot of an item. We dated, but never very seriously.

"Lisa, how are you?" I stepped forward as she hugged me.

Her companion stepped forward, and I immediately recognized Peter Daniels. Peter's brother was one of the deputies that had gone to prison after my parents' murder. He stood silent, so I ignored him.

Lisa, however, was gleaming, "I am fabulous. I am working for the Barnes County News. Editor-in-chief, right here. It's nothing big, but I love it."

"Congratulations, Lisa," I said as my eyes darted to her left hand. No ring.

"What are you doing in town?" she asked, "I thought you were some big city man."

"No, I am more of a wanderer now. I do a lot of traveling."

I noticed Peter still stood unmovingly.

He was determined not to acknowledge me, but then again I was returning the favor.

"So, Max, I heard you were working for The Memphis Daily?" Lisa asked.

"For awhile, I got very sick of the media game." I thought it was time to switch on the charm. "To be honest Lisa, you have it better here. No politics, no news slants, no loaded stories. I bet you run your own show."

She beamed with pride, "You bet I do. I have free rein in almost all cases."

"Did Mandy call you?" Lisa said unexpectedly. "I know you two were close."

I had hoped not to be drawn into this discussion here, especially with Peter standing there.

"What?" I asked as dumbfounded as I could sound.

"Don't kid me. The jail is right there. You haven't been in town in years, and then when Mandy is arrested you appear. I may only be a local reporter, but I am still a reporter."

"No, she didn't call me. "

It was the first time that Peter even stirred. He shifted as if he wanted to back away from us.

Lisa must have sensed it. "Well, we have to go. Why don't you stop by the office sometime before you leave?"

"It's a deal."

I walked across the street to my car. I decided to head to the boat. I didn't quite know where to go from here yet. I decided I should find a nice bottle of wine to take with me to Tom and Cathy's.

7

I had arrived promptly at seven. I had taken the time to stop and find a liquor store that carried a decent bottle of wine. I was lucky that a new one had opened in town that carried a 98 Jordan Cabernet Sauvignon. They only carried that one, and it cost me an exorbitant $80. However, a 98 Jordan Cab is like heaven on the palette.

Cathy enveloped me as I entered the Campbell abode. Cathy even tussled my hair like I was six. I didn't mind. She had always coddled me.

She had a new do on her hair. Cathy had always had long red hair. She had often been the envy of many other women in this town, and the object of affection of many of the guys who had gone to high school with me.

Tommy, their son, had always been teased about how the guys wanted her to spank them. Tommy had gotten into a handful of fights because of it. I missed Tommy. He was about two years older than me. He had wrapped his Ford Ranger around a tree. He had been racing along some curves when he tried to dodge an armadillo. I was only 16.

He was still alive in the gnarled blue metal of the little truck when Tom and Cathy arrived on the scene. Tammy Cloud, his girlfriend, had been sitting next to him in the truck. She had been pulverized instantly. Tommy cried aloud to his parents and hers how sorry he was.

The fire department tried desperately to cut him free. It took almost an hour. Tom and Cathy stood nearby in tears while they talked to their only son as he was dying.

Tommy told them that he loved them. He told the Clouds how sorry he was and how much he loved Tammy. He looked up into the night sky and closed his eyes. I remember standing back with my mom when he died. Cathy nearly collapsed. My father had rushed to his friends as we watched the horrible spectacle.

Less than a minute after Tommy died, the firefighters freed him from his car. Paramedics tried to revive him. He didn't seem to want to come back. I had never watched anyone die before that moment. I never encountered death before that night. I have never been able to avoid it since.

I enjoyed every minute of dinner. Cathy had made some of the best homemade lasagnas I had eaten in a while. However, homemade food was a rarity for me nowadays. She had warm garlic bread soaked in butter. We savored the wine and conversation.

After a delicious apple pie for dessert, Cathy left Tom and me in the den so she could clean the kitchen. Tom procured two

Cuban cigars from a humidor on his shelf. I gladly accepted. I pulled my lighter from its pocket prison and lighted my cigar. I slowly rolled the cigar so that it would evenly light.

"The bail hearing will be Monday morning."

I took a puff off the cigar, "Okay, I will post it."

"Not necessary. I talked to Judge Hurt. The hearing is a formality. Amanda Rawls won't have to stay with the Barnes County Sheriff through the weekend. Tomorrow morning, she will be released into your custody."

"Now if you lose her, then you will have to deal with Judge Hurt. It will likely cost you a mint. So keep up with her."

I smiled, "Don't worry."

"Oh, I'm worried. I don't want you getting in too far over your head. I am going to offer Charlie a deal. Maybe she can get off easy."

"Let's hope so. But she denies it. Didn't

even cop to self-defense."

"It's strange, this whole affair. Apparently Lofton just up and married Leigh Rozen."

"What do we know about Ms. Rozen?"

"She runs this 'herb' shop off Highway 7." Tom made little quotation signal with his fingers when he said the word "herb."

"Really?"

"I am sure she has some oregano and parsley, but I would bet she doesn't make her living on those."

"How long has she lived here?"

"A couple of years, I think. Jane Cay used to run the herb shop out there. It was legitimate then. I'm sure Leigh took all the legitimacy out of it."

"What happened to Jane Cay? I didn't know her."

"She moved here about six years ago. She came to me to check about all the legalities involved. She was outside the city limits so she didn't need a business license.

She had a small store and a garden where she got some of her fresh herbs. But she got married and moved to Little Rock, I think."

"Has Ms. Rozen had any legal issues since she's been here?" I asked.

"When the sheriff has to bust guys busting crystal meth labs all over the county, he doesn't go looking for someone who stays under the radar." Tom took a long drag on his stogie.

"I'm curious about something else, Tom," I asked as I fingered the ring on the cigar.

"Yeah."

"Aren't Cubans illegal?"

"Depends on who is around when you are smoking them."

I exhaled a gust of smoke with a laugh.

8

I woke fairly early the next morning at my new home, however temporary. At least it was early to me. I have never been fond of the mornings, so I try to avoid them as best I can.

The digital clock in the master bedroom read 8:32 a.m. I climbed into the shower and refreshed myself.

I had a lot that I wanted to do today. I found a cappuccino maker in the kitchen and proceeded to make myself a stout mocha. The kitchen was fully stocked, and I topped my mocha with whip cream. I climbed the steps to the upper deck. The morning air was revitalizing. After my coffee was gone, I finished dressing and headed up the dock to my car. The marina is only ten minutes from the town square, and I arrived shortly after nine.

I was hungry, so I proceeded to The Smokehouse. It was new; at least it wasn't here ten years ago. It had been a little bar called Philo's. I had never even been inside Philo's; being underage, I never went into bars. I always did my drinking down by the river.

I walked into the wood-paneled restaurant and found a table in the corner. I have always heard that breakfast was the most important of the day. I never miss it. Sometimes it might consist of cold chicken and a warm beer, but it's still breakfast.

As it turned out, this morning I wasn't going to eat breakfast. I was minding my own business trying to decide between bacon, eggs, and toast or bacon, eggs, hash browns, and toast when Lisa Day sat down beside me.

"Can I join you?"

"A little late to ask."

"Well, I have an idea. I want you to help me investigate this murder."

I looked at her. "No."

"Max, come on. We can help Mandy out."

"Lisa, I would really like to help you. But I can't today." I stood up and dropped two dollars on the table before leaving the restaurant.

I decided a nice, enjoyable breakfast was out of the question now. Thankfully, there are the two things with which no town can live, Wal-Mart and McDonald's. I don't think that it is a given fact, but I am certain that one could open a McDonald's in the middle of nowhere and it would not only make money but also create a community around it. So in keeping with community spirit, I visited the McDonald's that Hellenston was most likely built around for an Egg McMuffin and an orange juice.

After my well-balanced breakfast, I decided to head over to the jail. I was supposed to be able to take Mandy into my custody.

It took a little over an hour to get the paperwork shuffled. I have spent more time trying to rent a condo than I was getting a suspected murderer out of custody. By 11:15, Mandy walked out of the jail with me.

"I am going to take you to stay with me for now, okay?" I said as I opened the door for her to get into the convertible.

"Okay, but I need some clothes and stuff."

"I will get some for you after I drop you off at the boat."

"Boat?" she cocked her head questioningly.

"Yeah, I am staying down at Pryor's Bay on one of the houseboats."

She made an approving look, "Those are nice. But I can go with you to get my stuff."

"No," I was emphatic, "I want you to

stay put there."

Mandy remained silent in agreement, and then a moment later, "Thanks, Max."

I smiled at her and pulled the Bimmer onto the highway. I revved the engine and headed toward the marina.

The ride was quiet. Mandy seemed very contemplative as she stared off the road. I am sure that the trauma of it all seemed to be catching up. We got back to the boat, and I led her inside. She exclaimed with wonderment about the boats many amenities. I took her to one of the bedrooms.

"Now make yourself at home. There seems to be plenty of food and beverages. Just stay here, watch some TV, and get some rest. You are going to need it."

She walked back to the bow of the boat. "What are you going to do?"

"Well, I have to go get you a change of clothes, and I thought I would make a little visit to Herbs and More."

Mandy nodded.

"I will be back later. We are going to have a nice dinner tonight. Here is my cell number, "I handed a card to her. "There is a cell phone over there on the radio. Just give me a call if you need anything."

Mandy smiled and then surprised me with a kiss on the lips. The kiss was meant as a friendly peck, but it lingered a second longer that had been intended.
"Thanks," she said in a whisper before turning to go back to the bedroom.

I took a cue from a nagging feeling in my gut that this could be a bad idea, and I made a quick retreat. Outside, I could still taste her lips on mine. I felt a half smile creep across my face. I made my way off the marina and to my car.

9

Herbs and More was little more than a trailer at the end of long dirt road. The road appeared to be a private drive for the store that apparently was housed in an old tan trailer. I parked in front of the trailer and climbed out of the car. The dirt on the drive was dry, and each footstep I took created small clouds of dust.

I climbed the wooden steps of the porch. A hand-painted sign hung on the trailer that read "Herbs and More" in red paint. Beneath the large sign, there hung a smaller "Open" sign. Both of the signs looked as if they had weathered a tornado or two. I knocked on the door to the trailer.

As I waited for an answer, I glanced toward the woods where an overgrowth stood that I am sure was meant as an herbal garden. The soil had probably not been hoed or shoveled since Jane Cay abandoned the shop for her new love.

I knocked again. This time the trailer shook and creaked as its occupant was alerted to my presence. A minute later, the door of the trailer opened a crack.

"Yes," a voice on the inside said. A face then appeared in the door's crack.

"I was interested in some herbal remedies. I heard in town that you were the person to see for such concoctions."

She seemed hesitant, "Well, that depends. What kinds of remedies do you need?"

"Something natural, to relieve stress and boost energy," I flashed a smile and hoped it iterated the unspoken, "Know what I mean."

It obviously did, "You a cop or something?" She eyed the BMW sitting behind me. Her face seemed to light up as if my answer would not make much difference.

"No ma'am." She seemed to take me at my word and opened the door.

I stepped into the dingy trailer. The room was set up like a kid had decided to play shop. There were a few shelves standing around the room that looked like they had once held some goods. There were a few jars of dried herbs scattered around the shelves. The room where I was standing was obviously multifaceted. It contained the kitchen (if a busted stove, a mini-fridge, and a microwave count as a kitchen,) the bedroom, and a den that consisted of a fold-out couch and a television.

"I'm Max." I extended my hand.

"Leigh," she replied with a gust of breath that reeked of menthol cigarettes and cheap liquor. She was not unattractive, but unkempt. She had long brown hair that hung like a Raggedy Ann doll. She wore a tight Tim McGraw t-shirt that was meant to show off her breasts. I suddenly realized that she wasn't wearing any pants, and when she sat down I realized that she was without panties as well.

"So," I ventured, "can you help me out?"

"I am sure I can," she smiled, and I was surprised to see that she actually had nice white teeth. "Anything particular you are hankerin' for?"

"Something to create Ecstasy."

She stood up and again flashed the entire netherworld before my eyes. She walked to the back of the trailer. "Wait here."

I was still standing in the room. I glanced around the room. There was a cordless phone lying on the sleeper. An old VCR sat atop her television along with a stack of video tapes. I walked over and flipped through the titles. There were several porn videos, a couple of recent movies, and a National Geographic video on owls.

She was moving around in the back, so I decided to snoop a little more. There were several ashtrays filled with butts and roaches. She had hung some of her lingerie, if you wanted to count a latex teddy as actual lingerie, over chairs, and there were several condom packages and used condoms in her trash.

I moved over next to the couch where a table stood with a half empty warm can of Natural Light beer that had been sitting for a while. There was a drawer in the table. I paused and listened to her moving about. I decided to chance it; I slid the drawer open slowly. There were several pieces of paper and some notepads. I rummaged quickly looking for information. There was a yellow sticky pad with a phone number scrawled across. I grabbed the sheet and anything else that looked vital I stuffed into my pocket so I could look at it later.

I slid the drawer in and turned back as Leigh walked back down the tiny corridor.

In her hand, she carried a brown paper sack as if she were Alice giving Ralph his lunch before work.

"$250." She set the sack on the couch. I wasn't very familiar with the prices of drugs nowadays. However, $250 seemed steep to me. Perhaps it was simply the law of supply and demand.

I slid a roll of money out of my pocket and peeled away three bills, making certain that she saw how much remained. As soon as I handed the money to her, she expressed a sudden attraction to me. I am sure it was more to the dead presidents that I carried with me.

"So," she whispered as she sat down next to me, "would you be interested in doing any more business?"

"Not today, but I guarantee if this stuff is good, then I will be back for more."

She moved her hand up her leg brushing her shirt up to expose more of her thigh, "Well, I have more to sell."

I stood up and touched her shoulder, "I will keep that in mind." I picked up the sack and started toward the door.

The late Mr. Lofton's bride sure seemed to be coping with the murder of her husband. I got into the car and peeked into the bag. It was quite a little goodie bag. I set the bag down on the passenger seat and started the car.

As I put the car into gear, I noticed the curtains of one of the windows brushing open and Leigh Rozen peering through the window. She was running her fingers of her left hand over her breast. She tried to give a seductive smile. I waved at her as I pulled away from the trailer.

I touched the accelerator and sped back down the dirt road toward the highway. As I drove along, I pulled a few pieces of the papers I had extracted from the drawer. There were several telephone numbers on them.

I had a friend who worked in D.C. for

the F.B.I. He was a surprisingly good contact for information about these things.

I pulled my phone from my pocket and touched the hands-free button.

"Nikki," I responded to the prompt.

A minute later, I was connected to Nikki.

"Nikki, I need you to call John Woods."

"Sure thing, Max. How are things there?"

"Well, so far I am violating only three or four federal laws."

"If you can't be good, be careful, Maxie."

"Don't worry, if I can't be good, and I can't be careful, I will at least name it after you."

Nikki laughed.

"Ask John to give me a call on my cell phone. I need him to check some numbers for me."

"You got it," Nikki said in her soft, but

firm voice.

"Another thing. Can you FedEx my case to me? I need to get some of my toys."

"Sure, where to?"

"Ship it to Tom's house. I need it by tomorrow."

"It's done."

After I hung up with Nikki, I picked up the brown sack. I was about to toss it out of the car, but I hesitated. It wasn't the smartest thing in the world to carry that much dope, but it might come in handy as evidence. As long as it wasn't going to be evidence against me.

10

My next stop was going to be Mandy's house. Picking up her clothes was a great excuse to snoop around some. Mandy's house is about ten miles outside of Hellenston on the opposite side of the river. Mandy lived in her mother's house now that her mother had remarried and moved to Baltimore. It was the same house that she had lived in when we were in high school. I had some fond memories of our time together, and I was sure that my mental picture was accurate despite the years of fade around it.

Like so many of the houses and trailers on the outskirts of town, Mandy also lived down a long dirt road. There were a couple of houses when you first turn down the road, but for at least a mile there is nothing but fields and woods before one reaches Mandy's house. The fields were in the midst of turning from the summer green to the autumn gold. Several bales of hay were scattered about the fields, and they almost looked natural.

Mandy's mother had a lot of land surrounding the house that she had used to pasture show horses. However, after her mother moved to Baltimore, the land was unused. Mandy had a perfectly quiet residence with a lot of space and no one around to bother her.

Or to hear her? I was struck with an epiphany, so to speak. Who called the sheriff? The nearest house is at least a mile away. No one could have possibly heard anyone fighting, and a shotgun blast, even, would not wake anyone up that far away.

If someone was close by then, they could be either an excellent witness or else a very good suspect.

My first thought was the tire tracks; however, the police and ambulances would have created too many to get any good leads.

However...

I slid my phone out of my pocket and dialed Tom.

"Tom," I said as I got out of my car in front of Mandy's house. "Have you gotten the time of death for Mark Lofton."

"Around 1:30 to 1:50."

"So he hadn't been dead long before the cops showed, and according to Mandy she arrived only seconds before the cops." I walked around the front yard looking at the ground for something that may have been missed. "What time was the call?"

I could hear papers shuffling through the phone, "Hold on." A second passed, "The call came through at 1:56 a.m. Sheriff's deputies arrived at 2:01 a.m."

"Only five minutes after the call? They must have been close by when they received the call.

"Do we know who made the call, Tom?" I asked.

"It was anonymous. The call went to the desk at the sheriff's office. No ID."

"Tom, that doesn't make sense. Why call the desk and not 911?"

"Maybe they panicked.".

"Or maybe they wanted to call without being traced. What's the sheriff's direct number?"

"I don't know right off." He answered.

"Neither would the caller most likely. He had to look it up first, or he would have to at least know it."

Tom agreed, and I continued, "Tom, have you even been out to the crime scene. Mandy's house is at least a mile from any other house. She is at the end of a dirt road surrounded by acres and acres of fields and woods. Who would possibly be this far out here, much less at two in the morning? Even if they were, they should have still been around five minutes later when the deputies arrived."

Tom was silent. I evidently had a good point. Score one for me. I continued, "Who made the call? We have to find our caller."

"I will see what I can do," Tom said. "You really need to talk to Charlie about this."

"Why," I said, "you are the prosecution. I'm sure you don't want to send an innocent girl to the electric chair, do you?"

"Of course not."

"Good, besides I know for a fact that you are an honest man, and you want to see that the truth comes to light as much as I do."

"I will see what I can get."

Another thought occurred to me, "Did Mark Lofton have a car here?"

"No," Tom said.

"What about his clothes?"

Again Tom answered, "No, they

weren't recovered."

"Kinda strange, huh."

Tom's silence was again agreeing with me.

My mind was working in multiple directions. If someone had come in with Lofton, then how did they get inside? Of course, as I looked at the lock, the house would take me about six seconds to penetrate. In fact, it actually took almost twenty seconds and a paper clip to open the front door.

I told Tom I would call him later, and I slipped the phone back into my pocket. I walked up the path to the porch. The house was an old farmhouse. It had a wide front porch that was covered and allowed for folks to gather if they wanted. It was painted white, but the paint was showing signs of weather, and the roof looked to be in its last year if she was lucky. If I had to guess, I would say that Mandy had not spent a lot of time on upkeep.

Inside the house, the outline of the body was the immediate draw of my eyes. Lofton had been found lying in a heap near the beige couch.

The white carpet was stained with blood. My mental picture was a bit different on the inside. Mandy may not have spent a lot of time outside, but the inside was nicely decorated. The furniture was fairly new, and a 27 inch Sony television sat in an armoire with a VCR and DVD attached. There were several videos and DVDs stacked neatly on the shelf. I noted several titles: *Titanic, Blazing Saddles, Monty Python and the Holy Grail,* and all the *Star Wars* movies. Mandy seemed to still enjoy the same taste in movies that she had in high school.

I knelt down and peered at the room. I tried to envision the incident. Mark Lofton comes to the house. He wants Mandy to continue to be his lover. Not at all surprising considering the dismay that Mrs. Lofton seemed to be feeling earlier. Still, he comes over, intent on satisfaction with Mandy. He even takes off his clothes while he waits for her to get home. She comes home, and he pushes himself on her. She rejects him, and he gets mad and attacks her. But she showed no signs of being attacked. Besides it would be self-defense, and she could probably walk free and clear.

No, Mandy would have been honest about that. So Mark comes here and is shot by someone else. But how did he get here? His car would have been towed to an impound lot by now.

The problem is that someone wanted Mandy to take the fall for the murder. Their timing had to be right, but they still left gaps. The police arrive just as Mandy gets home so she hasn't had time to call 911. Her engine should have still been hot.

The cops have a suspect, and her prints are on the weapon. But not on the shells. I walked across the living room to a large gun cabinet. I remembered it being there when I

was dating Mandy. The cabinet hadn't
moved in at least twelve years. It had a glass
door that allowed me to see the former
location of the shotgun used to kill Mark
Lofton. I tried to open the cabinet. It was
locked. The box of shells was sitting at the
bottom of the cabinet.

I made my way to Mandy's closet and
pulled out some clothes for her. I didn't
bother with a bag. I just carried a handful
out to the car and put them in the trunk.

I walked over to her car that was still
parked silently in the driveway. The doors
were unlocked, not surprised in a small town
like this. I climbed into the car and looked
through the front seat. There were some
assorted receipts for gas and other items.
The gas gauge read full. Perhaps if I could
find a receipt for gas that Mandy got in or
around Little Rock, then she might add some
credence to her story.

I would have to ask her about it when I
got back to the boat. Something that simple

might save her.

It was all very bizarre. Mark Lofton was here without clothes or a vehicle. Why bother with the setup, though? If you wanted Mark Lofton killed, then it would be easy to put a bullet in him, and then to carry him deep into these Ozark woods and bury him. He would be missed, but a character like him could easily vanish from town when his wedding day approached closer.

Except, he suddenly got married.

What was he thinking? Leigh Rozen is not the best catch in these waters I am sure. Granted, she did have that trailer charm, and she wasn't hideous. But it didn't seem right. I wish I knew what he had been thinking.

Perhaps Mrs. Lofton can share some information about it with me. I suppose I should make my way back to her humble home. This time I should get to the point.

It took me another twenty minutes to get back to Leigh Rozen Lofton's trailer. It was 3:30 p.m. when I reached the turn off of the highway onto the little dirt road. I pulled up to the trailer and walked back up to the door. The door was open slightly. I knocked loudly.

I received no answer. I knocked again. I pushed the door open with my foot to see Leigh Rozen-Lofton lying on the sofa bed with a .38 Special in her hand. Her brains were on the drapes and window behind the sofa.

No doubt that she was distraught over the loss of her husband.

11

I stood over the sofa bed staring at the lifeless form draped across the sheets. The same bed had been folded up only a few hours earlier. Otherwise, the trailer did not appear much different than it had earlier.

There did not seem to be a sign of struggle. I made a rash judgment that the suicide was staged.

The blood on the wall behind her head was still wet. Blood coagulates in about four minutes, meaning that the killer was still near. I forgot the urge to search and opted instead to make a quick exit before someone decided to include me in Leigh Rozen's suicide pact.

I quickly jumped into my car and pulled it onto the highway. I raced the car to

60 miles per hour. With any luck, I could be across the county before anyone would find the body. I needed to call Tom. He could send the sheriff to the trailer.

I was still concentrating on moving away from the scene when a police cruiser appeared with its lights flashing. My heart leapt, and I glanced at the passenger seat where the brown bag I had bought from the late Mrs. Lofton sat. I held my breath, and the cruiser sped past me, on its way to the gruesome scene.

I waited until the car was out of sight before I tossed the brown bag into the ditch. I felt relieved to be rid of that little bag. Better safe than sorry, I thought.

I reached for my cell phone and dialed Tom's number. As the phone rang, I looked at my rear view mirror to spy the flashing blue lights crest the horizon behind me. My luck just ran short. The phone continued to ring as the lights raced upon me.

Tom answered.

"Tom," I spoke quickly, "Leigh Rozen is dead."

The police car was right behind me. I slowed as I pulled to the shoulder.

"What?" Tom replied, "Where are you?"

"Listen, quickly, I think I will be under arrest inside of a minute. If I don't call you back in ten minutes, then you had best meet me at the police station."

"Max, don't say anything until I get there."

"Don't worry," I replied.

I turned the phone off and stepped out of the car.

"What's the problem, sir?"

"Stop, and keep your hands where I can see them."

I obeyed as the officer moved toward me with his gun directed at my head.

"Turn around and face the vehicle."

I complied immediately, and the officer began to inform me of my Miranda rights.

His partner came around the car and began to pat me down.

"What's the problem?" I asked again.

"We need to ask you a few questions."

Both officers were standing behind me. One of them grabbed my shoulder and turned me to face them.

"Did I do something wrong?" I asked playing dumb.

"Possibly. A woman was killed, and we need some information."

"That's awful, but I don't know anything."

The first officer shuffled around my car, peering inside the window. The second officer whose nameplate read Burns remained in front of me. He was intentionally narrowing his eyes in an attempt to appear menacing. He wanted to strike me with fear, but he was almost trying too hard. I have noticed that it is extremely difficult for a nice guy to portray themselves as hard-liner.

"We need to take you to the station. Ask you a few questions."

"Am I under arrest?"

"Not necessarily."

"Fine, then I will gladly answer anything you ask here. I am happy to cooperate."

The first officer, whose name I had been unable to read yet, returned to the discussion. "We need to take you to the station in order to establish your involvement in this incident."

I glared at him, and I read "Matthews" on his silver nameplate. "I will be happy to follow you to the station."

Burns responded, "No, why don't you ride into town with us?"

"I don't think so. This is a BMW. I don't really want to leave it on the highway."

"It will be fine here. We can have it towed if you like, but it will be later today before you get it."

"Hope you know this is a waste of time.

I plan on calling my lawyer before I answer any questions."

The two deputies remained quiet as they placed me in the backseat. Luckily, I was saved the indignity of being cuffed.

Fifteen minutes passed since I hung up with Tom, and we were pulling into the parking lot in front of the station. Tom would be here shortly if he wasn't already. I couldn't wait. I am not immensely comfortable being a guest of Hellenston's finest.

My escorts walked me to the same room where I had talked with Mandy yesterday.

"Sit down here for a minute," Matthews ordered.

"I need to call my lawyer."

"Don't worry. You can." The door shut and then clicked as it locked. I sat down and pondered my current situation. I had a funny feeling that I had been intentionally placed in this predicament. The police had responded rather quickly to the murder of Leigh Rozen. It took at least ten minutes to get from the station to the trailer. Even if the officers were on patrol it would take a few minutes to arrive unless they were already in the area.

It seemed rather obvious that whoever called the police was most likely the perpetrator himself. I would further venture a guess that he had seen me and my car. The officers must have had a description of my car, or else why come after me. It was feasible that a neighbor had called the police if they saw me leaving the scene. However, that
would also indicate that they would have known that something was amiss to find me suspicious.

No, it seems only logical that whoever shot Leigh Rozen in the head was close enough to see me. The real question was, "Where was he hiding?"

Luckily for me, if the murderer was the

one calling the police, then it was highly unlikely that he would bother testifying against me.

Things were beginning to take a little form, at least in my opinion. The door opened, and a tall, skinny man walked into the room. I recognized him immediately as Scott Gaither. Gaither had been a deputy when I left ten years earlier. Apparently, he had finally made it to the sheriff. He was in his mid-thirties with dark auburn hair and a matching mustache. He had been an honest cop, at least ten years ago. Though his honesty had little to do with his attitude about me.

"Maxwell Sawyer, this is indeed a treat." Gaither swung the door shut.

"How's it hanging, Scott?" I leaned back in my chair.

"Not too bad. So, Sawyer, what are you doing back in town? I thought you were off living on daddy's money."

"Can't a guy get homesick?"

107

Gaither leaned forward, "You've heard the saying, 'You can never go home again.'"

"So I hear," I sat up straight. "Well, tell me Scott, what it is that I can do for you?"

Gaither stood and paced around me, "What you were doing out at Leigh Rozen's place?"

"Where is my attorney?"

"I believe that he will be here shortly."

I folded my hands together, allowing my fingers to cross, and I rested my chin on my thumbs. My elbows rested on the table. "I suppose that unless you wish to chat about the Razorbacks or the weather, then we can wait for him to arrive."

I broke my gaze at Gaither and stared at the wall. He nodded to the officer behind me, who immediately exited the room.

"Just so you know," he sat down across from me, "I have a witness that saw your car at the trailer."

"How about this heat? Awfully hot for October, huh?"

"That's okay, Sawyer. We don't have to talk now. But I figure you were trying to cover up for your girlfriend. I hope you don't mind being able to sit behind bars."

"So, what do you think of the Hogs this year? I bet they will be able to make it all the way. But it's only October. Probably too early for anyone to count their chickens."

Gaither became silent, obviously annoyed. I leaned back and propped my feet on the table. The room was very silent for several minutes before the door opened, and Tom walked into the room.

Gaither looked slightly relieved, "Can we get started now?"

"That would depend. What are you holding Mr. Sawyer on?"

"Suspicion of murder. I just want to ask him a few questions."

Tom looked at me, and I gave him a shrug.

"Okay," Tom replied sternly, "however, if you get out of line, Scott, I will not allow him to answer."

"Fine," Scott came back before turning to me, "Mr. Sawyer, why were you at Leigh Rozen's place?"

"Was I? I don't even know Mrs. Lofton."

Tom looked at me sharply, as Gaither raised an eyebrow.

Gaither, who had obviously noticed my verbal lob across the net, chose to ignore my remark for the present. "We received a call reporting a shooting. The caller identified your car and yourself as leaving the premises. Care to explain why you were there?"

Tom shook his head, "He doesn't have to answer that."

"No, Tom, that's okay. I am going to have to stick to my story I have a feeling someone is pulling your leg, Scott. Who is your witness?"

"I am not about to tell you who my witness is." Gaither stood as defiantly as he could.

"Fine, I will be glad to see his statement, or at least let Tom peruse it for validity."

"That will take some time." Gaither's stance wavered.

"I can imagine. I think that I have tired of this chat. Can we go, Tom?"

Tom stood, "Scott, do you intend to book him?"

Gaither shook his head, "Not yet."

I stood to leave, and Gaither grabbed my arm, "Don't worry, Sawyer. When I find my witness, you'll be back here."

"Scott, you forget yourself. You said 'find'"

Gaither countenance flashed annoyance at my observation of his slip.

"Aren't you a little curious about what happened to Ms. Roz...Mrs. Lofton?"

"Not really, I didn't know her," I said as I exited the room. Then I turned, "but if I were to guess, I would have to say someone

111

put a very hot piece of lead through her head."

I turned and followed Tom out the door.

Outside Tom decided to scold me, "You are walking a thin line. Care to share some of the details with me."

"I suppose I could share some of the details over a cocktail. Your treat."

"No problem," Tom laughed, "I'll be sure to expense it."

We ventured across the square to a small pub that had opened since my last visit. The inside was a bit gruff by Memphis standards, but for a small town, it was really rather nice.

We found a seat at the bar, and Tom started, "Okay, let's hear it. What happened at the trailer?"

I ordered a Maker's Mark on the rocks, "I was there twice today. Earlier around 12:30, I had a talk with her. Scoped her out a bit. You know, asked a few questions, bought some drugs, turned down her sexual offers, and left."

"You didn't actually buy drugs?"

"You bet your sweet bippy I did. Luckily I had the good foresight to toss them from the car after I found her later."

"When was that?"

"About 3:30. Just a few minutes before I called you."

Tom sipped a cold Budweiser, "I did some quick checking before I came down. The sheriff's department got the call at 3:34. A second call came through describing you and your car."

"911?"

"No, the call went directly to the desk. No caller ID and the caller did not leave his name."

I lifted the bourbon and took a swallow. "Whoever our caller is, he has to be our killer. He was still there when I left. I'm just not sure where."

I glanced at my watch. It was almost

seven. "I have a theory I want to check tomorrow, but I need to get back to my car. I have to get some dinner out to the boat for Mandy."

"So, how's that working out for you?"

"Purely platonic," I smiled.

"Sure," Tom grinned slyly as I swallowed the rest of my drink.

12

Tom drove me back to my car, which was still sitting on the highway. As I approached the car, it was obvious it had been searched. Not surprising, but I wondered who had done the searching.

"I'll see you tomorrow, Tom. I am expecting a package to be delivered to your house sometime in the morning."

"Alright, Max. Be careful, you don't really know what you are getting yourself into. This isn't a game."

"I am always careful."

I drove the Bimmer toward the boat. I stopped at the grocery store and picked up some fresh shrimp and the makings for a fabulous Cajun shrimp Alfredo on a nest of angel hair pasta. I thought Mandy could enjoy a nice meal.

A few minutes passed, and I was walking aboard the boat to find Mandy sleeping on the couch. The television was playing quietly. I found the remote, and the screen went black. I put all the groceries into the fridge.

Mandy slept soundly as I draped a blanket over her. Deciding to put the shrimp on ice, I found some bread and made myself a peanut butter and jelly sandwich.

I munched my sandwich and wandered behind the bar. I shook up a very cold Manhattan and poured it smoothly into a martini glass. With my cocktail in one hand and a sandwich in the other, I walked up to the top deck.

The moonlight ricocheted off the water as it gently pushed past the hull of the boat. The river murmured with the sounds of boats taking fishermen out for their prey.

The upper deck had several comfortable deck chairs scattered across it.

On one side was a rocking love seat. I rested slowly and sipped on my Manhattan, mulling over the day. The night was warm and windy, and the stars glittered brightly across the sky.

I often find a little quiet meditation will help soothe the raging bulls running through my head. It only takes a few minutes of silence for me to relax. An hour passed, and my Manhattan had long since been drained.

I sat quietly listening to the sounds of the water splashing against the boat. I was jerked from my symphony of solitude to the unpleasant tones of my cell phone. I jumped to my feet and slid down the ladder on the port side of the deck. I scrambled through the bridge to the counter where my phone was singing loudly.

"Hello?" I said.

"Max, it's John."

"Hey, John, how's it going?"

"Pretty good. And you?"

"Not bad, but I need a favor." I

proceeded to share the recent events with him. After I brought him up to date, I asked him if he could check the numbers I had absconded from Leigh Rozen's trailer.

"Tomorrow's Sunday," John said, "but I will see if I can pull a few favors and get anything for you by late tomorrow. Might be Monday."

"John that would be great. I owe you again."

"Don't worry; I am sure I will collect sometime."

I told him goodbye, and he promised to call later. Mandy was still asleep, and I decided to retire myself. I slipped quietly into my berth. The solitude and the Manhattan had done wonders for me, and I quickly drifted into a comfortable sleep.

13

I awoke in the dark. A soft scent floated in the air, and I realized that Mandy was sleeping next to me. My eyes adjusted to the dark as I lay there quietly. I sat up at a sound outside, like something moving on deck.

I slid out of the bed, and my bare feet touched down on the carpet. Mandy stirred slightly as I stood. I moved out of the room as quietly as possible. I stood in the living area. Everything was silent, but I felt very wary after the day.

I decided to go out on deck, but I didn't want to use the sliding glass door. It made too much noise on a quiet night. I went back through the bridge and out the small door beside the ladder that I had slid down earlier.

I slowly pulled myself up the ladder. I froze when I heard rustling on the top deck. I continued slowly, lifting my head just above the deck.

The moonlight cast shadows across the deck. The rustling sound occurred again, and my eyes darted. Beneath one of the deck chairs, a small raccoon scurried. It moved into the moonlight, and I breathed a sigh of relief. I pulled myself up and placed a knee on the deck.

A glint of moonlight reflected in the corner of my eye before a blow forced me down on the deck. Stunned, I tried to scramble to my feet. A black figure moved toward me, and I jerked upward as a foot struck me in the stomach.

I fell to the floor and rolled toward my attacker. I thrust my arm out blindly. Luck guided my hand, and I struck his right leg. He lost balance for only a second. I scampered out of his reach.

My attacker recovered before I could

get to my feet. His fist came down hard against my cheek. He stepped back, and I wasted no time jumping to my feet.

My feet did not even have the chance to get firmly planted when I saw the business end of an oar sweeping toward me. I caught the entire force of the blow in my chest. My back struck the railing, and a second strike from the oar sent me flailing overboard.

The ice cold water surrounded me, but I was barely able to feel it. A few seconds passed before I was fully conscious of what had happened.

I kicked as hard as I could toward the surface. My hands found the hull of the boat. Another second later, I was gasping through the surface of the water.

I could hear the tapping of footsteps on the dock. My assailant was escaping. I grabbed the railing on the side. I pulled myself up. Two taillights were racing toward the highway. I could only make out

the shape of a truck before I collapsed onto
the deck.

14

My eyelids lifted, and light flooded my pupils. I squeezed them closed and tried to open them slowly. A paramedic stood nearby with a deputy. I was lying on the couch. Mandy was sitting at the table when she saw me wake.

"Max," she moved to my side. "How are you?"

"Sore." I was sore. I felt every muscle in my body screaming in agony.

The deputy noticed me as I sat up slowly. He motioned toward me, and the paramedic rushed to my side.

"Careful now," the paramedic, who was only a 20 or 21-year-old blonde kid, spoke softly as if his voice might be causing me more pain. "You seemed to have taken quite a beating. You are lucky, though. Nothing seems to be seriously damaged."

"Doesn't quite feel undamaged."

He smiled, "You'll probably have a giant bruise on your chest tomorrow."

"I already feel it."

The deputy, who had stepped outside, returned with Scott Gaither in tow.

"Well, well, Mr. Sawyer. Had a kinda interesting night, huh?"

I nodded.

"I have to say," he continued, "I was not too happy to get a call in the dead of night that a murder suspect was almost killed. A little coincidental?"

"A little."

"So, Sawyer, did you get a good look at your friend?"

"No, it was dark, and he caught me by surprise. I think he was over six feet tall, but I wasn't really able to tell."

"Was he black or white?" Gaither asked.

I shrugged, "I think he was white, but I

couldn't say. He drives a pickup truck."

"Figures. Not a lot to go on, Sawyer. Did he say anything?"

I shook my head.

Gaither looked toward the deputy. "I called Tom Campbell for you. He said he would be by in the morning."

I nodded my response.

"Billy, here, thinks you are going to be okay, but he wants to take you to the hospital for an x-ray." Gaither cocked his head to the flighty paramedic, who still stood with his smile.

"I think I'll be fine," I stood up slowly. Nothing felt broken, but I could tell I would be sore. I had been in worse fights, and I never let one get me down.

"You may still have a few cracked ribs," Billy said with great disappointment in his voice.

"It won't be the first time then. Right now I just want to get back into the bed. The last thing I want is to spend a couple of

125

hours in an ER."

I looked at my watch. It was almost half past four. I felt utterly exhausted, and I only wanted to get back to sleep.

"Can I go to bed now?" I asked.

Gaither eyed Mandy, "I imagine so."

I narrowed my eyes, "Then you'll have to leave."

"I'm gonna leave a car here until the morning, just in case."

I nodded, and Gaither and his troops slowly exited the boat.

After the dock had cleared, the cops were still milling around the parking lot for a few minutes before all of them left, except one.

Mandy moved over next to me, "How are you feeling?"

"Just a little sore. Nothing too bad."

"This is all my fault. I am so sorry."

"No, this isn't your fault. You never asked me for anything. I brought it all on myself."

"Max..." her voice was very soft.

"Besides, think how good I will feel when it stops hurting."

Mandy smiled and leaned in to wrap her arms around me. I held her for a minute.

"Why did you come to help me?" She held her head against me.

"I don't know. I had no choice. We have always been friends. I couldn't let..."

I was interrupted when her lips pressed against mine. She wrapped her arms around my neck while we kissed. It was an incredible kiss, and for a moment I was completely lost in her arms.

After a minute, she pulled away. She gently pulled me toward the bedroom. For the second time that night, my brain was several seconds behind my body. I was following her when I stopped.

"Mandy, you...We have been through a lot tonight. I don't want...Let's sleep on it. Make sure you feel okay in the morning."

Mandy's face drooped, "I'm sorry, Max. I..."

"I didn't say I didn't like it. I just don't want to wake up tomorrow and find your opinion of me different. You are too vulnerable. After tonight, I am even vulnerable. Let's not be rash."

She moved away from me, "Okay, I'll sleep in the other room. I just didn't want to be alone."

I really felt like a heel. "I think, if it's okay with you, that we... Well, I just, I think we had a rough night, and I don't like to jump into anything too serious. Let's take smaller steps."

"Okay" Mandy looked confused, and rightfully so, because I was utterly confused myself.

I kissed her on the cheek. She smiled, and we stood. We walked into the bedroom. I passed out quickly from sheer exhaustion

.

15

I felt great until the morning arrived. I had given up any hope of getting a lot of rest by eight-thirty. Mandy was still curled in my arms. My chest ached, and I slowly slid out of the bed. A large purple bruise had formed on my chest.

I stumbled to the bathroom for a long hot shower. I climbed into the shower and turned the handle all the way into the red. As the hot water pelted my skin, I sat down in the tub. I was hoping some heat therapy would soothe some soreness. I had a lot of questions to get answered today, and I had no intention of letting anything like a little soreness get in the way.

I leaned back in the tub letting my lids slide closed. The water bounced off me, and

I began to relax. After a moment, I drifted into a comfortable doze.

I awoke a few minutes later when the door opened. Mandy stuck her head in slightly. "Excuse me."

"It's okay, come on in."

"I just wanted to check on you. Feeling okay?"

"Just a little beat down," I smiled.

"Want some aspirin?"

"No, thanks. I was thinking about going to see Mark's house. Where he lived before he married Leigh Rozen."

Mandy sat on the toilet, "I want to go with you."

"Not a good idea."

"Too bad. I am going with you."

"Mandy..."

"I have a key."

I lost. "Okay, but you drive."

The curtain popped open, and Mandy leaned in and kissed me quickly.

"Want some food?" she asked.

"Sure, a little something." I answered and Mandy smiled as she exited the bathroom.

I was feeling much better, though I was still very sore. I pulled myself to my feet. Clouds of steam hung about four feet off the floor. I found a towel and wiped the water from my purple chest.

I emerged from the bedroom donned in a white pullover and black slacks. I slipped into a black leather jacket.

I hoped that at some time today I might come across my attacker. He would probably get quite a shock to find me up and about. Perhaps my determination might put a bit of fear into him. Of course, it could also get me killed.

I found Mandy in the kitchen. She was slaving over a few pieces of toast. She handed me two slices slathered in butter. We ate quietly.

"Thanks for breakfast," I said after finishing.

She smiled, and I felt it might be a good time to ruin her mood with some nasty questions.

"Tell me. Did Mark give you any indication he was having an affair?" I was right. I watched her mood swing down quickly.

"No, I had no idea. I know it makes him sound like trash, but he always treated me like he loved me. He always brought flowers. He was very romantic. In fact, he insisted we get engaged, not me. I never pushed it at all. Never really thought about it, until he asked."

I studied her carefully. She had gone through a lot in the past couple of weeks.

"Why the sudden change? Leigh Rozen was no catch, and there didn't seem to be a lot of love lost when he died."

There was some trivial item I was missing. It seemed to be escaping me now.

"Did Mark use drugs?"

She shook her head, "He did some pot,

I know. He never did anything else that I know of."

"Let's go see what's at his house," I rose slowly and stiffly from my seat.

Mandy snatched the keys off the table and we walked off the boat.

16

Mark Lofton lived in a rented trailer on a lot on the edge of Hellenston. I sat in the passenger's seat feeling my muscles ripple with aches and twinges. Twenty minutes later we arrived at the trailer. Lofton's nearest neighbor was half a mile away. That was good for us. At least with a key, we weren't breaking and entering.

It was obvious that the police had already done a fairly thorough job of sifting the place. With Mandy's help, we were able to locate Lofton's more valuable possessions. Unfortunately, the trailer was spotless. Anything of any value to us had already been taken by the police.

We walked back outside empty-handed. Mandy leaned against the car, while I strolled around the trailer. I noticed a yellow circle in the grass. The garbage can have probably been there. No doubt it was now evidence.

I walked around to the back of the trailer. On the back, there was a single door with a small flight of wooden stairs. There were several piles of junk lying around the yard.

Less than a hundred yards behind the trailer was a line of trees. The forest looked deep from where I stood. I walked toward-the trees. The grass was wet, and my shoes quickly developed a small coating of water.

I looked up from my shoes and into the woods. I glimpsed something in the distance. I walked toward the woods, and as I came closer I saw a hole that had been used as a personal landfill. It was far enough from the trailer to be easily overlooked.

Mandy must have come around the trailer for me. I heard her jogging behind me.

"What is it?" she asked.

"That must be Mark's dumpster."

Her eyes lit up, "I didn't even think about that."

The pit was about ten feet across and probably another ten feet deep. There was trash piled up about five feet. The walls of the pit were blackened by smoke. Apparently, Mark burned his trash every so often. Luckily, it looked like it had been awhile since his last bonfire.

I climbed down into the pit. My feet sank slightly into the surface of the rubbish. I knelt down and began sifting through Lofton's refuse. It didn't appear to have been searched through yet, and I was willing to bet the police had not noticed it on their initial search of the property.

Empty bottles of cheap beer gave away Mark Lofton's easily pleased palette. Most likely the beer was meant to complement the vast array of frozen TV dinners that he had been consuming. I was wondering if Lofton had ever eaten a home-cooked meal.

Mandy climbed down and began to help me pan for clues. For twenty minutes, we sifted and sorted the trash. We were growing nastier as we continued to wade through the muck. Then I struck gold.

I wanted to shout "Eureka" when I found a slimy check stub stuck to a Sears sales flyer. I peeled it carefully away and examined it.

"J.T.'s Club," I read the name of the account. It appeared to be a paycheck from a club located in Little Rock.

"Did Mark work down there?"

"I don't know. I thought he was working construction."

I peered at the check; it was dated only three weeks ago.

We continued to poke through the trash for another fifteen minutes before we decided to give it up. We were both smelling fairly rank and in need of a shower.

17

Tom was waiting on the dock when we arrived back at the boat. He expressed his disgust as we approached.

"Did you get beaten up by the garbage man, or what?"

I gave him the biggest, sarcastic smirk I could muster. "Been busy this morning."

"How are you feeling?" he asked seriously.

"Very sore, but I've been worse."

"I brought that over," he pointed to a FedEx package that he had left on the deck.

"That's mighty kind of you."

"No problem," he replied. It was fairly evident that he was avoiding any contact with Mandy.

"Want some coffee?" I offered.

"No, thanks. I have a lot of work to do."

Tom reached for my hand and gave Mandy a very curt nod. I let Mandy go on board, while I walked Tom to his car.

"So, have you heard anything new?"

"Not really. Other than Scott's prime suspect was nearly killed last night. I'm a little worried, Max."

"Don't sweat it, I'm a big boy." Tom often felt obligated to fill in as a father to me since my dad was murdered. Since his own son also died, I think that I also filled a role he needed.

"Max, be careful. Don't forget that the police in this town may not be bad, but they don't exactly have a short memory."

"Neither do I," I said as my lips turned up.

Tom turned toward his car with great resignation.

"Tom," I blurted, "one more little favor. What do we know about Leigh Rozen's background?"

"Nothing much," he replied, "especially that I can share."

"Prior arrests? Jobs? Family? Friends? Something must be there for you to share."

"I'll let you know later."

I sighed at the obstinate old man, "Fine, I am going to go to Little Rock for a little while today, so I'll call you later."

"Max, don't get too involved here. You already had someone try to drown you. You don't want to get killed for a high school sweetheart."

"No, I don't want to get killed, but I don't plan on it either."

I turned and left Tom to his own grumbling. I still felt slimy and smelly, and I really wanted a shower.

18

When I boarded the boat, I could hear the shower running in the back. I took my package into the bedroom. With a quick cut from my pocket knife, I had the box opened. Inside was a large black suitcase that I quickly pulled onto the bed.

I snapped the clasps and lifted the case open. My collection of neat gadgets was kept inside. Many of the items I had obtained in some fancy spy shops in New York, including a small parabolic mike that could pick up voices several hundred yards away. Some of the smaller more complex bugs and listening devices came from other sources in different law enforcement agencies. I did a quick inventory, and I lifted up a false bottom to reveal a secret compartment. There I stored a chrome 9mm Glock with several magazines of ammunition.

Once I was completely satisfied that my collection was complete, I replaced everything and closed the lid. The shower had gone quiet now, and I could hear Mandy moving around as she dried off.

The door opened, and Mandy walked out wrapped in a towel. Her hair was still wet and mussed from her towel. Water droplets still held their position on her bare shoulders, and while the towel covered all the important parts, there was quite enough to send pulses from my head to my toes. She smiled at me as she passed out of the room, and I wondered if she was getting at me intentionally.

I decided two things right then. First, a cold shower was probably exactly what I needed right now, and second, I needed to leave Mandy here while I went to explore J.T.'s Club. Somehow, though when I got

into the shower, I just couldn't bring myself
to keep the water turned to ice cold; instead
I twisted the knob until I had steaming, hot
water pouring over my sore muscles. I was
beginning to feel them stiffening from the
over-exertion I put them through last night.

19

It took some convincing to get Mandy to stay on the boat. She was determined to go to Little Rock with me. I reminded her that the police might not take too kindly to her traveling outside of the county. She reluctantly agreed.

I left Hellenston the same way I had entered two days earlier. As I left the city limits, I noticed a gray Mazda Protégé in my rear view mirror. It was far enough back that I only noticed it. However, after half an hour had passed I noticed that it was still back there. I slowed my car to 45 miles per hour, and the little gray car remained about a quarter of a mile behind me. I was almost certain that I was being tailed.

I reached into the back seat, where I

had set my black case before I left. I quickly unlatched it. I felt beneath the false bottom until my hand grasped the cold metal of the Glock. I pulled it out and laid it on the passenger seat.

I am not a fan of violence; however, in certain cases; I will admit it is the only answer. After last night, I wanted to be sure I had the only right answer.

I continued to drive and waited for the right moment to reshuffle the cards. A sharp curve took me out of the view of my tail for several seconds. I slammed the brakes and slid the car to a stop on the shoulder of the road.

I grabbed the pistol from the passenger seat and quickly got out of the car. I slipped the gun into my belt at the small of my back. I leaned against the car, just as the Mazda came around the curve. It swerved quickly, and I gave a gentle wave.

The gray car stopped several feet in front of mine. I watched as Lisa Day stepped

145

out slowly.

Surprised, and relieved, I smiled, "Are you following me?"

"Not really," she meekly denied like a child caught red-handed.

I cocked an eyebrow, "Because I will have been glad to tell you where I am off to. If you want to know."

Lisa's lips curled and pressed together in resignation, "Well, after last night, I thought you might be into something interesting."

"Last night?"

"You were attacked," she stepped forward and slapped my chest with the back of her hand. I winced in pain, and she smirked. She had a tiny bit of revenge for the humiliation I had just heaped on her.

She continued, "I thought you might actually be on to something if you are stirring up hornets like that. After all, the police are keeping an eye on you since Leigh Rozen's suicide."

"So what do you know about her suicide?" I asked.

"I know enough to guess it wasn't a suicide. So unless you killed her, then there is another murder here." She pulled a pack of cigarettes from her jacket. She slid one from the pack and slipped it between her lips. "I figure though that if Scott Gaither can't pin it
on you, then he'll let it go as a suicide. Don't you agree?"

"I wouldn't know right off."

Lisa turned away from me as she lit her cigarette. She pulled a breath of smoke in and exhaled. "Well, it might interest you to know that they are fingerprinting her trailer right now. I hope they don't find anything incriminating on you."

"Lisa, I really have to be off. I do have someplace to go today..."

"Max Sawyer, you are not about to ditch me. I did let you get to second base with me in ninth grade. You owe me."

147

I smiled; she had let me make it to second base. I could still vividly remember.

"Lisa, I do appreciate it, and I do owe you. But one day I will make it up to you with a home run. Today, though, it is a bit too sticky a situation for you to get involved. I know you noticed how the local mod squad seems to be gunning for me. You don't want to be guilty by association."

"Don't worry about me. Scott wouldn't think of taking me down with you. He doesn't like you for sure, but in a way he owes you. He wouldn't be sheriff if Sheriff Hanson hadn't gone to prison."

Lisa was skirting the issue, and I was grateful. There are some people who have no idea what it was like. How hard it is to forget the bloody scene. Finding Leigh Rozen shot is bad enough, but when a seventeen-year-old boy walks into his house to find his mother and father lying lifeless in a blood-soaked bed, it is a memory that haunts you forever. I have to shake the image from my head constantly.

"Lisa, I really have to go."

"Tell you what," she continued to argue," why don't you let me go along with you. I have some more information that you might find interesting."

"Not today." I tried to be firm, but I was still remembering my crush on her in ninth grade.

"Fine," she stated firmly, "I can follow you."

"Follow me," I laughed, "I spotted you before we left Hellenston. You could never keep up with me in that."

She seemed offended at my derogatory comments about her little Protégé. She did not, however, let them stop her from trying to tag along. "I'll make you a deal. I have some information about Mark Lofton that I am willing to bet you don't have yet."

I was really getting worn down by her persistence, "Okay, what's the bet?"

"I'll tell you in twenty minutes. I would

hate for you to have a change of heart and leave me here."

"No deal, if you are bluffing me then I'll find out after it is too late to kick you out without feeling terribly guilty about leaving you on the side of the road."

"Okay, then the bet is this. If the information I have is old news to you, then I will let you have your home run hit."

I smiled. I couldn't help liking Lisa. But still, I don't like giving in so easy.

I leaned in gently toward her ear and whispered, "What makes you think I even want a chance at bat."

"Because my pitch has greatly improved since ninth grade." I resigned my position. She had me speechless, a condition I rarely find myself. I moved to the other side of the car and opened the passenger door. She smiled graciously as she slid into the car. I shut the door and moved to the driver's side. I pulled the Glock from my belt as I climbed into the car.

Lisa eyed the pistol, "Planning to shoot me, huh?"

"Only if you had been the one that sent me swimming last night." I placed the gun beneath my seat.

She nodded, "Did you see who attacked you?"

"Yeah, he wore a very large boot. We might be able to make a cast from the imprint on my chest."

I started the car and raced it onto the highway. Within seconds the needle of the speedometer was quivering around 60 miles per hour. I reached forward and gently pushed the disc sticking out of the CD player back into the slot. Then the sound of a trumpet filled the car and the road around us.

"What's this?" Lisa asked.

"The great Miles Davis. Just listen and enjoy."

"This is old people music. My dad listened to stuff like this."

I looked at her and sighed, "I guess good taste doesn't get passed down in the genes."

Lisa cocked her head, "Thankfully, nothing much got passed down to me."

"So, how are your folks?" I asked.

Lisa stirred in her seat, "Dad left Mom right after graduation. I've seen him three times in the last five years. He didn't even come to my college graduation. He cleaned out their bank accounts and left Mom with a ton of debt. I had to work my way through school, and Mom moved back to Atlanta with my grandparents."

"Oh, I see. Why did you come back here then?"

"It's still home to me. I have too many memories to just leave."

"I guess I have too many memories to come back."

"You know, Max. Memories are something you can't just run away from. You have to learn to live with them."

I shrugged, "Maybe. I like to ignore them."

"Don't you have some good memories? Friends? Girlfriends? Dogs or cats?"

I thought about it, "I suppose."

"Try thinking about them."

The next half hour passed quietly as I sped along the country roads with Miles blowing his horn. I finally decided it was time for her to pay her fare.

"Okay, time to pay the piper."

Lisa squirmed, "Okay, this came from a confidential source, so I can't tell you where I got the information. It seems Mark Lofton had a lot of money passing through his bank account. Something to the sound of $100,000 has bounced in and out of his account in the last three weeks."

"That's a lot of money for a guy who rents a trailer and is married to a drug dealing whore. Where is it coming from?"

"No idea. They are all cash deposits. They stay for a day, and then they are

153

transferred out again."

I pondered for a second, "Any idea where it might come from?"

"Not really. I checked with John Mead. He owns the construction company that Lofton worked for. He said he didn't have that kind of money to come up missing. Besides, Lofton hasn't shown up to work in three weeks."

I mused quietly. I did find it very useful, but at the same time, I really didn't want her to know that she had the upper hand on me. So I held my tongue and my thoughts for the moment

However, Lisa seemed a bit anxious about sharing, and I decided to pump her for some more information.

"I remember John. Dad did a little work for him, but I don't think that he liked him much. I seem to recall that he used to run around with the girls."

"He still does," Lisa chimed. "The latest rumor is that he is running around with

Tonya Woods."

"I don't remember her."

"Probably not, she graduated a few years after us. She moved here when she was a senior. She was a bit of a...well, a whore."

I am often amazed at how down and dirty women can be about each other.

"So she developed a bit of a reputation," I replied, "Anyone particular?"

"I suppose just about everybody," Lisa sounded almost venomous, and I could guess that Tonya had stolen someone from beneath Lisa.

"So, how long had Lofton worked for John Mead?"

"According to John, it was on and off for two years."

"So, did you know Lofton?"

"Yeah, kinda. We saw each other out."

I slowed the car as we approached the turnoff. "What did you think of him?"

"I suppose he was nice enough. He

155

liked girls quite a lot."

"Made his rounds, huh? Recently?"

"I'd say. I saw him out last Wednesday with a girl."

I let out a slight laugh, "Not exactly the faithful newlywed. Who was the girl?"

"Well, I really am not sure who it was."

The answer was aloof, and I remained silent, letting my brain register.

20

We drove in silence. I had already
pulled Miles Davis from the CD player,
replacing him with Louis Jordan. I let
Jordan's jazzy trumpet and velvet voice pass
the time as we drove into Little Rock. It
didn't take me long to find J.T.'s Club. It was
a small looking place on the outside.

Lisa and I walked through a large
wooden door. A blonde sat behind a counter
in a tight, slender silver dress that showed
nearly every roll and wrinkle she had
acquired. A strong odor of cheap perfume
floated in the air.

"Ten dollars," she flashed a large, fake
smile. I gave her fifteen, and then I led Lisa
through another door.

The inside of the club was dark, and

bright strobes and spotlights flashed around the room quickly. In the center of the club was a large round stage where a shapely, nude girl danced awkwardly to the blaring sound of David Lee Roth singing "Jump."

Sunday was apparently not a busy day, and only a handful of patrons were seated about the club.

"Are you sure you want to stay?" I asked Lisa.

"Yes."

I would have preferred to have been alone. I enjoy my elbow room, but Lisa was obviously along for the ride. I am sure I could make the best of it

"Okay, follow me and keep quiet."

We found a table against the wall. It was set back from the stage. It was far enough from all the action to provide a wider view of everything. I leaned back and took a moment to absorb everything in the room. A place like this could very easily have a hundred different things occurring simultaneously. It is always best to get a lay of the land before trying to trek it.

The bar ran along one wall between two columns. The left column was the barrier between the bar and a flight of stairs tucked into a small hallway. A large steroid induced bouncer stood guard in front of the hall. A girl stood chatting with him. Behind the bar, another girl in a tiny tuxedo shirt and tights tended to the drinks. A man who had obviously been drinking for a long time was being escorted past the guard by a buxom blonde in a bikini.

"Want a beer?" I asked Lisa.

"Not really, how about a margarita?" She pulled another cigarette from her case.

"I doubt it." I stood and walked to the bar. I didn't bother to order the margarita but opted for a trendy Smirnoff Ice for Lisa and a Budweiser for myself. The bartender gave me twenty ones in change, and I strolled back over to Lisa.

I handed her the Smirnoff Ice and the

ones. "Go tip the dancers, and look like you are enjoying yourself."

"What?"

"I want to get a lap dance, and poke my nose around a bit."

"Fine," Lisa turned her beverage up and drained a good portion of it. She stood up and moved away from me.

I scanned the room till my eyes settled on one dancer standing next to the bar. She seemed to be a bit bored with the slow Sunday crowd. Perhaps, I could quickly entice her.

I made quick haste to the cold beer in my hand, and I carried the empty bottle back to the bar. I ordered another beer and slid a ten across the bar to the bartender.

"Keep the change."

I glanced toward Lisa, who was making progress with the dancer on stage. Lisa was standing onstage, and the dancer had both of her hands sliding around the inside of her skirt. Lisa smiled awkwardly, but her eyes shot me an evil look. I couldn't help smiling.

"You're late," a voice slurred behind me.

I turned around to face a man standing behind me. "The party shtarted without you," he said to me. He was in his mid-forties with dark hair and mustache. He reeked of beer and bad taste.

I gave him a smile in response, but he continued to mumble under his Budweiser ladened breath. "I jusht want to have fun, but shum folks have no idea."

I could feel myself being sucked into this guys spiel. I tried to step away, but he moved closer. "I got a limo outside," he said in order to impress me.

I gave him a smirk and said, "I'm not going to sleep with you."

He laughed at my retort as if he had thought it up himself. "I could have any of these girls," he crowed.

"Got that much cheese, huh." I was tired of his crap.

"Hell, yeah. Wanna get a couple upshtairs?"

I ignored him. I turned my beer upward and. A hand touched my arm gently.

"Hi there," a raspy voice came softly.

I turned my head to see the girl I had eyed earlier. She smiled seductively, and I was certain that she had practiced that smile until she got it just right. I thanked the gods that now I had an excuse to move away from this drunk.

"Hello," I replied before swigging another mouthful of beer.

This mistress pressed closer to me, and I inhaled the aroma of jasmine that came no doubt from her skin.

"My name is Trouble," she whispered in my ear. Her tongue lingered on the lobe of my ear, and I could feel my knees tremble. I am after all only human, and she was, after all, a very beautiful woman whose breasts were pressed tightly against me and whose tongue was mapping out the curves of my ear.

I took a deep breath and pulled away, "Charmed, I am sure."

Her smile melted from seductive to gentle. "What's your name?"

"Max," I replied, "Can I buy you a drink?"

"Actually, I was hoping to get naked with you." Her seductive smile returned as her fingertips began where her tongue stopped.

"Someplace private, I hope."

She stood up and seductively wagged her finger for me to follow. Trouble escorted me past the guard and down the hall next to the bar. I continued to follow her up the stairs past another bouncer sitting on a stool next to a jar full of dollar bills. JT's was prepared. If any vice cops got past the entrance, then there were two separate sentries ready to relay the message. This room was where anything illegal or unorthodox probably occurred.

The room was full of love seats; each one set to itself and angled so that one could not view the activities occurring at another seat. The room could be full, but no one would have any idea what was happening five feet away.

Trouble directed me past several empty seats to one in a corner that I imagined might have been her own personal space.

"What do you want?" Trouble asked as she removed her top.

I pulled a hundred dollar bill from my pocket, "Information."

Trouble was taken aback, "What?"

"I need some information about this place. Have you worked here long?"

"Are you a cop?"

"No, I had a friend that worked here."

"I've been here about a year," Trouble said as she snatched the bill from my hand. "Who's your friend?"

"Mark Lofton."

"Mark. Oh yeah, Jeff fired him a few weeks ago."

"Really. He was also murdered Thursday night"

She looked shocked, "Oh no. Who killed him?"

"I don't know yet. They think his fiancé killed him.

"Leigh?"

"No, his other fiancé. How do you know Leigh?"

Trouble seemed happy to share some gossip, "She was Jeff's wife. I heard Mark ran off with her and stole some money from the club."

"Really, is Jeff the owner?"

"Yeah, Jeff Thomas."

"Oh, JT. But that doesn't sound like Mark. He was supposed to get married to another girl."

"That didn't seem to stop him. I think he has been up here with almost every girl here. Not me, though."

I was certain her integrity could be brought into question; however, I decided not to concern myself with anything so obvious.

"Well, Mark used to be a good guy. He did like to party a good bit. Used to do some rolls with him."

"Yeah," Trouble said, "he always had something. That's how he got along with most of the girls."

"Really, so how much did he steal?"

"I heard several thousand," she slid her hand over my crotch, "but I don't want to talk anymore. Don't you want to have some fun?"

"Not now, would Jeff have killed him?"

"Oh, I wouldn't think so. Who knows? People do some weird things for money."

I looked at her and wondered if she caught the irony in her own comment. "How did you get into this business?"

"Oh, I used to be a nurse," her story began. She talked for almost half an hour about her drug addictions, her forte in taking money for sex, and how she wanted to quit and move back home to Alabama, where her four-year-old daughter lived.

21

After Trouble had finished my "private dance", she gave me a kiss on the cheek and promised me she would leave on the first bus tomorrow to Alabama. I wished her my best but knew that if I came back next week she would still be doing this. We walked past the guard, where I dropped a five into his tip jar.

I went back downstairs where I found Lisa sitting with another dancer and a fresh Smirnoff Ice in her hand and a half burned cigarette smoldering in an ashtray.

"Having fun?" I asked.

Lisa turned, "Oh yeah. This is Lavender."

"Hi," I nodded to Lavender.

She squirmed a bit, "I have to get back

to work."

She left quickly, and I looked at Lisa, "Did I interrupt something?"

"Yes, you did. Did you have fun?"

"Absolutely, it was very productive. How did you make out?"

"Cute," Lisa sneered. "I made some friends and found out a little about Mr. Lofton."

"Great, let's get out of here. I'll buy you dinner and we can share the gritty details."

We stood to leave, and Lisa suddenly froze, "Max, that's Paul Grace."

I turned in the direction of her eyes. A white-haired man in his late fifties was walking out of the door on the right of the bar with another man in his thirties.

"Who is Paul Grace?" I asked.

"He is the porn king of Little Rock. He is organized crime in Arkansas. He owns a ton of strip clubs, and supposedly several escort services and whore houses in nearly every county north of Little Rock."

I watched the two men talking and walking across the room. Oblivious to the naked women and patrons around them.

"We have to follow him." Lisa was excited.

"No," I said sternly, "the last thing I want is to end up on the wrong side of a guy like that." That wasn't exactly the truth. I did not want to end up on Grace's wrong side, but I did think I needed to know more about him.

"But he may be connected. This could be a real story."

"Or a one way trip in a coffin. Besides one mystery at a time. The other guy interests me."

"That's Jeff Thomas."

I smiled at Lisa. It seemed she did get some good information from Lavender.

Thomas and Grace were moving toward the exit together. Lisa looked at me as they walked out the door.

"Okay, I guess we get to follow them."

I stood up, "Stay with me."

I guided Lisa to her feet with my hand at the small of her back. I wrapped my arm around her and pulled her close.

"Max..."

"Just shut up and start acting now," and I pulled her toward the exit.

A moment later, we were standing in the open air. Paul Grace and Jeff Thomas were standing next to a car in a serious discussion.

"We have to hurry," I mumbled, and I stumbled in the direction of Grace and Thomas. The looks on their faces said a lot. Grace was angry, and Thomas was fearful.

We continued to move past them when Grace's voice rose. "I want it back. Find out where my money is." He suddenly quieted as if he realized he was getting too loud. Thomas looked as if he were consoling him on the loss of a loved one.

A bustle of people came out of the club, and the two men stopped talking. Grace turned and walked toward a tan Lexus sedan. I hurried Lisa to the car, as Grace's Lexus left the parking lot. Jeff Thomas turned to go inside. He stopped and pulled a pack of cigarettes from his pocket. He lit it and casually walked inside the club.

Grace was already gone, and Lisa seemed disappointed that we didn't follow him.

"How about dinner now?"

She smiled, "Okay."

We drove downtown and found a nice Italian restaurant. We found a nice booth in the corner. I ordered a bottle of Pepperwood Grove Pinot Noir while we perused the menu. Lisa was quiet and it gave me a minute to mull over a few things in my mind. It took only a second to decide on the bow tie pasta with shrimp and cream sauce.

It did seem that the money that had bounced in and out of Lofton's account had probably come from Grace and Thomas. An excellent motive for a porn king to kill someone. But it was apparent Grace was still missing his money. It also seemed too obvious. This was interesting.

I had to see if Grace was involved, but even more important, I had to find the money.

22

I wanted to get inside Jeff Thomas' office. Unfortunately, I either had to take Lisa along for the ride, or I had to drive an extra hour in order to take her back to her car and get back here. I was a little pressed for time so I decided to count her in on the job. Besides it wouldn't hurt to have someone know what I was planning on doing, in case the plan backfired.

After dinner, we drove back toward J.T.'s Club. I gave Lisa a rundown of my intentions, which would only break a few laws.

"What are you hoping to find?" Lisa asked.

"Your big story," I answered as I pulled into a parking lot a couple of blocks from the club. "If Grace is connected to Thomas and if Lofton stole money from Thomas, then one might wonder if Lofton stole Grace's money. Porn kings don't often like having their money stolen from them. That kind of thing can cause problems."

"So are you looking for a paper trail?" she asked.

I parked the car and got out. I reached into the glove compartment and pulled the handless attachment for my cell phone. I connected it to my cell phone. I normally cannot stand the thing. It screams pretentious.

"What do you have planned?" she asked.

"I want you to stay here in the car. Drive around for a bit. Just stay within a few miles of the club so we can get out of here quickly."

I slipped the receiver in my ear. The earpiece was extremely small so it was unnoticeable. The microphone was the size of a button and was easily hidden.

"How long will this take?" Lisa asked.

"It's about three hours before the club closes. I figure that Thomas will leave before closing. If I can get into his office before the club closes then hopefully I can be out within a couple of hours."

"If not?" Lisa asked.

"If not, then I hide until everyone leaves, and then I search the office."

"It's a good thing you fed me before we sleuthed around. Otherwise, I might have gotten grumpy before we were finished." Lisa pulled her cell phone out of her purse.

I smiled and whispered, "I always feed a girl before I let her commit larceny."

I got out of the car and walked around to the passenger side. I opened the door and motioned for Lisa to get out.

"You might as well drive. I don't want the doormen to notice the car, so you are going to drop me a little closer to the club. I will walk from there."

Lisa nodded and quickly moved to the driver seat.

As she shut the door, I asked her, "You do know how to drive a stick, right?"

"I can drive anything with wheels."

"Okay," I conceded, "but watch the shift pattern. BMW has a very tight pattern, and the reverse is opposite what you are probably used to."

Lisa started the car and backed out onto the street. She seemed to grasp the shift pattern quickly. At least, she didn't give any indication that she couldn't figure it out. However, Lisa struck me as the type to never admit to failure.

She drove two blocks down the street before I told her to stop. I dialed her number. It rang once, and she turned it on. I quickly slipped out the door. As soon as I shut the door, Lisa continued down the road.

"You're clear," I said casually into the mike.

"Good luck," she answered.

J.T.'s Club was in a fairly industrial neighborhood. Most of the buildings were warehouses and businesses that closed up at five. Some were vacant buildings. There were few lights illuminating the area, and the few that were lighted cast dark shadows across the empty parking lots.

The club was an almost welcome sight of lights and activities after a block of dark quiet. I casually walked across the parking lot to the door. There was a different doorman checking for minors. I walked up and flashed my license. He checked the age and pointed me inside. I walked inside and found a different girl taking money for cover charges.

I wasn't in the mood for any socializing, and I wanted to avoid both Trouble and Lavender. However, once I was through the door I was caught by a girl who was looking for a drink. The beer girl stood by the door, and I ordered two Bud Lights. I handed the stripper her beer.

"Wanna dance?" she asked me.

I gave her a shrug, "Not right now. I just want to drink my beer."

She took the rejection nonchalantly and turned away.

I rolled my eyes and said loudly, "You're welcome for the beer."

She turned back, "Oh, thanks." And she walked away.

I walked around and scoped the building's layout. The office that Grace and Thomas had walked out of was on the other side of the bar. I moved through the throng of people grouping around one of the satellite stages close to the bar.

"Lisa, can you hear me?" I wanted to check in regularly with her to keep me at ease.

"Yeah, barely. I am getting a lot of noise too."

"Not much I can do except ask the deejay to turn down the music."

"That's okay. I don't want you to draw

179

suspicion."

I smiled to myself and said, "Yeah, cause my talking to myself seems normal."

"Somehow, I doubt anyone is looking at you. Unless you went into the wrong club."

I made it across the room where I could have a clear view of the office door. It was down a short hall. It also looked extremely difficult to access without someone seeing me. I moved a little closer and took a swig from my beer. I could probably get in quickly without too much unwanted attention as long as the door wasn't locked. Then I would have a problem. It would not take me long to pick the lock, but it would take long enough that someone would notice.

"Lisa," I said.

"Yeah."

"It's going to take a minute to get inside. The office is too visible."

"You need a distraction?" she asked.

"If you have one handy, yes."

"Give me a minute." She hung up on me.

I sat down at a table and drank the rest of my beer. I had no sooner set the empty bottle down than did a waitress appear wearing black stockings and black strapless teddy.

"Do you need another beer?" she asked.

I nodded, and she turned to head to the bar.

I waited for my beer and my distraction patiently. I scanned the room and counted four bouncers standing around looking buff. Adding the one at the door and the two watching the private dance area gave me a total of seven. Maybe eight, if one was on a break somewhere. I did not see any sign of the two dancers that Lisa and I had talked to earlier. It's possible that they had already gotten off, or they could be upstairs entertaining some businessmen. As long as they didn't see me, I felt safer in remaining anonymous.

The phone buzzed, and I slid my hand down quickly to answer it.

"You should have a distraction in a minute."

"What did you do?"

"I called the fire department."

The waitress returned with my beer. I paid her without tipping. I didn't want her rushing back to me every few minutes. Then I waited.

I didn't have to wait but a couple of minutes when the music stopped and the deejay came over the speaker.

"Everybody please listen up," he announced, and the entire club began looking around questioningly.

"The fire department has arrived and asked us to evacuate quickly due to the report of a fire."

The girls and patrons quickly began milling about aimlessly. The deejay continued speaking, "Please exit calmly. We will continue selling beer in the parking lot. This shouldn't take long, and we can get back to partying."

The crowd began moving toward the door, and I made my move to the office. I pulled my set of picks from my pocket as I walked toward the door. I gave a quick knock and received no answer, so I proceeded to pick the lock.

It took only a few seconds to line the tumblers up, and I opened the door and slipped inside as the rest of the crowd pushed through the exits. I relocked the door and hit the lights.

The office was grimy. There was a desk in the corner with a computer on it as well as a large collection of papers. A couple engaged, no doubt, in marital relations adorned a calendar on the wall. A file cabinet was sitting beneath the calendar. A small copier sat next to the file cabinet. The other wall had an armoire with a 35 inch Sony television in it. A large overstuffed couch sat opposite the armoire.

I decided to go for the file cabinet first. I pulled the drawer and was pleased to find it unlocked. I opened it to find the employee records. I flipped through the folders until I found Lofton's file. I pulled it and looked through it. It read that he had been fired, but made no mention of as to why. His date of hire was six months earlier. His last day worked was nine days ago. His marital status stated he was single. Otherwise, there was nothing of interest in it.

I flipped through several more folders. Most were records of the dancers and bartenders. I found a couple of folders for a bouncer or two, but none contained tax records. Only a few photos of the bouncers in flagrant delicto with girls I could only assume were dancers.

The next drawer really was just as interesting. Unfortunately, it was not helpful either. It was filled with pictures of Thomas with several of the dancers and a couple of the bouncers. Apparently, Jeff Thomas likes to play for both teams.

The third drawer was financial records. I quickly moved through the records. Some were tax records. I found a copy of the business license stating the club operated under a company called Orion Incorporated. There was no more paperwork on Orion Incorporated.

I looked through the last drawer and found only some personal papers belonging to Thomas. Most were credit card bills and statements. Thomas was probably using money from the club to pay his debts.

"Max," Lisa's voice sounded in my ear. I jerked in fright, having forgotten that she was listening to me move around.

"Yeah," I answered in a hushed tone.

"Everyone's going back into the club."

"Thanks," I replied. "Great distraction, by the way. You'll have to tell me about it later."

"Finding anything?"

"Not really."

I moved over to the computer. I hoped there would be some e-mail or message that Thomas had forgotten to erase. I had my doubts but it was a chance. I booted the computer and waited for the system to come online.

I began to rifle through the desk drawers while I was waiting for the system to boot. So far, I found little more than a collection of paperclips and some staples. In the side drawer, I found some papers and a Smith and Wesson .45 hidden beneath them. I closed the drawer and glanced at the screen. The Windows symbols popped up indicating the computer had booted up.

I started on the email icon on the desktop. I opened the program and clicked on the first mailbox.

"Checking your email?" a voice said.

I looked up to see the office door open and Jeff Thomas standing there with one of the muscle bound bouncers.

"Crap," I muttered under my breath, and I replied as drunkenly as I could sound, "I was...uh... looking for the bathroom."

"Did you find it on my computer?" he asked scornfully.

"I...just thought I would check my email," I offered.

"Jason," he said to the chunk of muscle standing behind him, "let's see if you can convince him to rethink his story."

I didn't have to rethink my story. I was pretty sure my story, and not to mention my body, was too thin to hold up to Jason's idea of interrogation. When Thomas and Jason stepped into the door, Thomas pushed it closed. They stood between me and my only way out. I decided that honesty might be prudent considering the current state of affairs.

"Okay," I confessed, "I am looking into the murder of Mark Lofton. It's been alleged that he embezzled some money from this club. That might give you motive, Mr.

Thomas."

"Are you a cop?"

"Yeah," I lied, thinking honesty was often overvalued.

"Got a badge, officer," Thomas asked.

"Not on me, but my backup outside will be happy to raid this club if you want."

I was hoping Lisa was hearing me, but so far, I had gotten no response.

"I don't think we have to worry about that. Jason, get him out from behind my desk."

Jason moved toward the desk with an angry look of someone who really enjoyed salting slugs as a kid. I really didn't want to take another beating so soon after my last, but Jason outweighed me by at least a hundred pounds, and it appeared that it was mostly muscle.

"Let's reconsider this," I pleaded.

"I did," Thomas said.

I grabbed the drawer to my side and yanked it open. My hand curled around the

.45 in it, and I raised it quickly. I trained the sights on Jason, who stopped mid-step and stared down the barrel. I flipped the safety off and gave a big grin.

"I told you to reconsider," I said.

"You won't get far," Thomas said.

"Long as I get out of this office."

"My guys won't let you out of the club."

I shrugged, "There are a lot of witnesses out there. I don't think you want to cause a scene."

"I doubt that will happen. Even if you do, we can just mark you up as a crazed drunk."

"I'll take my chances," I said as I motioned them to move out of the way. I backed up to the door. "Did you kill Lofton?"

"When I get my hands on you, you can ask him personally."

"Good hunting then."

I opened the door and left the office. I

189

shut the door and began swiftly walking
toward the exit.

"Lisa, where are you?"

"I'm about a mile away."

"Get here quick. And be ready to
leave."

Jeff Thomas and Jason came out of the
office behind me. Thomas was motioning to
the other bouncers. He was right they were
going to block the main entrance. I decided
it was time for an all out run. I put a few
tables between myself and Jason, who was
coming up on me quickly.

I located an exit sign at the back of the
club. It looked like a clear run if I could do it
quickly. I bolted toward the exit. Jason
pounded the floor behind me. Another large
bouncer was coming over the stage at me. I
stepped onto an empty chair and jumped
over a table in my way. The other bouncer
shoved the empty tables aside. I changed
direction and I ran across the satellite stage
where a blonde had stopped dancing to

watch the action.

"Excuse me," I said as I rushed past her and stepped onto a table full of beer. The two men leaned away from the table as it teetered over spilling beer bottles onto the floor. I charged for the exit.

"I need a ride," I said hoping Lisa could hear me.

"I'm in the parking lot."

"I'm going out the side exit," I screamed as I approached the door.

Suddenly a bouncer appeared to my right only a few feet away. I pulled the clip from the .45 and tossed it toward the crowded tables.

I then tossed the gun to the bouncer who froze in surprise before he caught it. I took the extra second to hurl through the exit. He had regained his composure and followed me through the door. I put all my energy toward sprinting toward the curb when I saw the silver shape of my BMW slide into view.

Lisa had dropped the top and I dove into the open car. The tires screamed as she floored the gas. A shot rang out as she bounced over the curb and hit the street. The tires gripped the street and we shot away from the club.

I peered over the back at the group of bouncers and Jeff Thomas watching our retreat. I leaned back and sighed in relief. I didn't know if they would give chase now or not, but I was willing to bet that as long as Lisa didn't slow down, we were safe.

"You sure know how to make friends," she said.

"Yeah, I guess I can consider myself forever banned from that place," I said, "I will have to add it to the list of places I can't go back to."

"You've been banned from other clubs?" she asked.

"Just Disneyland and Graceland."

"Should I ask why?"

I just smiled and shook my head.

Blood Remembered

Douglas Pratt

23

I wanted to get some more information on
Paul Grace. Lisa had given me the basics,
but she really only seemed to know what she
had seen on the five o'clock news. Austin
Knox had been an old high school friend,
but he now worked as a reporter at Channel
Seven in Little Rock. I had wanted to call
him after Mandy stated she had been with
him the night of the murder. I hoped he
might be able to give me some more detailed
information about Paul Grace's activities.

Once I let Lisa off at her car, I decided
to give Austin a call. I hadn't talked to
Austin in over four years, so it took a minute
to track down a number through directory
assistance. I dialed and waited for an
answer.

"Hello."

"Austin, this is Max Sawyer. Sorry, it's so late."

"Max! How's it going?" His voice perked up, "You calling about Mandy?"

"Yeah, you heard, huh?"

"The state police called me late Friday to ask me about her. I don't think I was able to help her much."

"Don't worry; I am working on another angle. In fact, I need some help."

"Absolutely," Austin said.

"Mark Lofton seemed to be neck deep in some serious problems."

"Really," Austin's voiced picqued with journalistic curiosity.

"Yeah, but let's keep this quiet for now. Off the record, if we want to help Mandy."

"Sure, what do you need from me?

"I think Paul Grace is involved. I know he is a bit of a gangster, but I need to know some more dirt on him. Any connections he has to J.T.'s Club or its owner, Jeff

Thomas."

"Paul Grace!" Austin seemed surprised. "What have you gotten yourself into?"

I slowed the car as I turned toward the marina.

I continued to explain, "I don't know how involved he is, but I have a good idea that it is probably more involvement than I would like."

"Max, throw me a bone. What's going on? How much trouble is Mandy in?"

I sighed, "Mark Lofton was working at J.T.'s Club recently. I suppose as the manager. Anyway, there was an undetermined amount of money stolen from the club. Paul Grace seemed extremely concerned that his money had not been found. The buzz is that Lofton stole the money."

"Can I have a little time?" Austin asked.

"Don't take too long."

I hung up with Austin as I parked in the

marina lot. I climbed out of the car and stood quietly in the moonlight. The night air was cool, and the stars reflected brightly on the river.

I started walking toward the boat. A sharp, loud crack resounded from the woods near the parking lot. My head swung quickly, and the hair on my neck stood on end. I scanned the dark woods for any movement. I saw nothing, but my instincts were certainly on red alert.

I was suddenly overcome with the desire to not have the living crap beaten out of me in my sleep. I moved back to my car and pulled the pistol from beneath my seat. I walked cautiously toward the boat, holding the gun so it was obvious to anyone within 100 yards.

Once I was on the boat, I turned back toward the woods and watched for anything. I knew I was probably over-reacting, but I was still sore from last night's thrashing and my 100-yard sprint through the club.

Mandy was watching television when I came through the cabin. I had slipped my gun into my waistband. I didn't want to scare Mandy too much.

"What did you find out?" she asked.

I sat down next to her. "A lot. I'm just not sure what to do with it yet."

Mandy straightened on the couch. She turned off the television. I opted to leave Lisa out of the tale, but I gave her the main gist of the events. I told her about the club, the drugs, the girls, and the money. She sat and stared blankly as I talked.

"How long has he been working there?" her eyes watered.

"I don't know. For a while I think."

A tear welled in the corner of her eye before sliding down her cheek.

"I didn't know him at all."

I put my arm around her. She curled up in my arms and quietly cried. I sat quietly stroking her arms as she cried.

After a few minutes had passed,

Mandy's tears had stopped. I looked at my watch. It was nearly eleven, and I could feel the entire day catching up to me. I was beat.

"Why don't you get some rest?" I told Mandy.

"How about you?"

"I think I need a drink."

Mandy tugged at my arm, "No, I don't want to be alone. Don't leave me."

I could feel the cold steel of the pistol. I was anxious with the idea of someone outside waiting to catch me asleep. However, I was too tired to resist, and I followed Mandy to bed.

24

I awoke some time later. The soft glow of the clock showed it to be about three o'clock. I felt immensely refreshed. Mandy lay next to me, her bare arm resting on my chest. My mind clicked along like the reel on a fishing rod. I had an idea in my sleep that was now about to breach. Mark Lofton's bank account, his sudden and recent nuptials to Leigh Rozen, Jeff Thomas, Paul Grace, and Mandy. They were all swimming together.

The stripper thought Lofton had only stolen a few thousand, but according to Lisa, there was almost a hundred grand floating around Lofton's bank account. The differences were astronomical. How much was really stolen? Half a million? More?

Mark Lofton may have had a few mental flaws, but anyone smart enough to steal that much money surely wouldn't just put it into his own account. Unless he wasn't smart enough to steal it. If Lofton didn't steal the money, then the money in his account was a ruse. An illusion. The real money was somewhere else. In the words of the great detective Sam Spade, someone may have played Lofton for a sap. In my experience, only a woman could play a man like that.

I slid Mandy's arm off my chest. I sat up slowly on the bed and reached for my clothes. I dressed quickly and quietly slipped off the boat.

25

I pulled into the driveway to see the sign for Herbs and More. I had an inkling that perhaps Leigh Rozen had married Lofton and then helped (or encouraged) him to steal the money.

Leigh Rozen may not have been the cracked-out whore she appeared. She was probably privy to information that her ex-husband did not realize. Mark Lofton could easily have been the patsy for her to relieve her husband of assets that alimony would not have given her.

Unfortunately for her, someone probably came to collect. Since I found her so quickly, I hoped the killer didn't have time to get it. The biggest flaw in my logic was a lingering question. Why would the killer alert the police to my presence at the scene? The police might find the money. Unless the money wasn't here, or it was hidden where the police would never find it.

If the money wasn't here then this trip would be fruitless. On the other hand, if the money was here then it was most likely not near the house. Besides the house was roped off as a crime scene; I wouldn't want an obstruction of justice charge levied against me.

I got out of my car and let my eyes adjust to the dark. I reached into my back pocket to retrieve a small Mag-Lite. I began canvassing the field behind the trailer. I had no clue exactly what to be looking for, but I still continued to look for it. I was betting that whoever killed Leigh Rozen had come from the back side.

The tree line bordered the field about a hundred yards behind the trailer. As I got closer, the light flashed on my quarry, an overgrowth that had been trampled. The brush concealed a trail that was probably used by four-wheelers or dirt bikes. This county, like many rural areas, had trails like this one zigzagging from one place to another. As a kid, I used to spend hours and sometimes days hiking through the woods along similar trails. Some of these trails skirted mountains along valleys for miles. This would easily have provided access to the trailer without being seen from the road.

I had travelled less than 50 feet into the woods when my flashlight illuminated something just off the path. I stepped across a thorn bush and knelt down. A cigarette butt lay atop a dead leaf. I lifted it to examine it closer. In tiny script around the filter was the name, Dunhill.

I stood and looked toward the trailer. From this spot, there was a clear view of the trailer and drive. Now I was certain I had a clear view of Leigh Rozen's killer, Charlie Nichols.

I was confused. I had seen no

connections to the lawyer. Of course, I had
not seen any firm connections to anyone
else. I began to feel I had been chasing the
wrong rabbit.

The moonlight sprayed across the field
casting eerily beautiful shadows. I clicked
the flashlight and let the shadows surround
me. My heart skipped as I saw a figure in
the field approaching.

I dropped to my knees and peered
through the brush. I realized that I had left
my gun in the car, and I mentally kicked
myself.

Whoever was out there was coming
toward me. I sighed with relief when I heard
my name shouted.

"Max," the voice belonged to Lisa.

I stood up and snapped the flashlight to
spread light toward the path. I weaved my
way back to the path and walked out of the
woods.

I pocketed the cigarette butt, deciding
to hold back until I determined why Lisa

205

was out here at four in the morning. Lisa trudged through the tall grass toward me.

"You aren't going to try to shoot me again?" Lisa asked.

"Not today. What are you doing here?"

"I couldn't sleep. I wanted to investigate here to see if I could find anything."

"Like the money?"

Lisa tried to act surprised, but the game was over for us. Lisa was along for the ride whether I liked it or not. In hindsight, I think I liked the idea of having someone along to offer another perspective. "Yes," she said, "it occurred to me that Mark might have left the money hidden with his new wife. Maybe Paul Grace had them both killed."

"Except," I interrupted, "that he still seemed extremely concerned about finding his money. I doubt he would have killed them without getting it back first."

"Well, it could be to prove a point.

Don't steal from him."

I pulled the cigarette butt from my pocket and handed it to her. "I think I know who killed Leigh Rozen."

Lisa peered at the butt and said, "Dunhill?"

"Unusual brand," I replied, "Charlie Nichols smokes them."

Lisa's eyes widened in surprise, "Where did you find it?"

"Back along that trail," I flashed the light toward the trail head.

"I think he may have used this path to get to the trailer without anyone noticing him.

"Where does it go?" Lisa asked.

"I'm not sure. How do you feel about a little late night hike?"

Lisa smiled, "That's exactly how I lost my virginity."

I laughed, "I heard it was under the stage in high school during the second act of a Midsummer Night's Dream."

Lisa smirked, "No, that was something altogether different."

"I knew I had missed my chance."

Lisa took the flashlight from my hands and headed in the direction of the trail.

"Don't kid yourself," she said over her shoulder, "You never had a chance."

I stepped in line behind her and shot a retort her direction, "That's not what I told the drama department."

"There you have it. That explains how I got 'under the stage.'"

I chuckled as we entered the dark woods. Crickets and frogs were singing loudly to us as we marched through the brush.

"Why Charlie Nichols?" Lisa asked.

"I have no clue."

"What about the money? Does he have it?"

"I haven't seen any connections to him and the money."

Lisa sighed, "There must be something.

We will have to find it."

"We may have to start at square one."

"At least," Lisa said with assurance, "there might be enough contrary evidence to get Mandy off the hook."

"Too bad her attorney is our prime suspect."

We hiked through the woods for nearly 45 minutes. Suddenly the trail opened into a clearing. Tire tracks and ruts crisscrossed the clearing so that there was no grass or vegetation. The clearing was surrounded by trees except a small opening that allowed the cars to get here. A second passed, and car lights passed on the other side of the trees.

"I know where we are," mumbled Lisa.

It felt familiar to me, but I wasn't sure.

"That's Highway 16," Lisa pointed to where the car had just past us.

"Right," I said, "the movie theater is down the mountain there. This is a prime make-out spot."

"So I hear."

I smiled at Lisa.

Lisa started to walk around the clearing. "So he parked here," she said to herself.

"Probably so."

"He knew the trail was here. Knew where it leads."

I nodded, "He planned this out. He had to know his car could only be seen by someone in this clearing. It's virtually invisible from the highway."

"Perhaps we can find someone who was here. There are always kids coming in and out of here."

"No one would have noticed an empty car. Besides Leigh was killed in the afternoon, it was probably deserted until later." I wanted to look around. Try to find another cigarette or something more tangible.

We searched in the dark, but our quest only unearthed two pairs of panties, three dried up condoms, an empty fifth of Jack Daniels,

and about ten assorted beer cans and bottles.
This was the only evidence that someone
had an extremely good time back here.

26

After our fruitless search ended, we decided it was best to get back to the trailer. We trudged back through the woods. The night was slowly fading into the early morning. By the time we reached the trailer the sun had begun to rise.

Once we arrived at our cars, Lisa said, "Since you bought me dinner last night, how about letting me buy you breakfast?"

I looked at my watch. It was 5:46 a.m. I was a bit tired, but also hungry. On top of that, I have a rule: Never refuse a beautiful woman's invitation to breakfast.

"Where are you going to take me?" I asked.

"The Red Rooster. Just follow me."

The Red Rooster had been the breakfast

spot for most of the early risers in
Hellenston since before I was born. Jean and
Marty Durange owned the diner that sat just
off Main Street behind the courthouse.
Marty did the cooking, and Jean did the
serving. A slew of their kids and grandkids
had worked there over the years.
I had a strong fondness and memory for
Marty's French toast. Dad and I would grab
breakfast there on Saturdays before going
fishing down the river. I hadn't eaten there in
over ten years. I didn't realize how hungry I
actually was until I started to drive. I
suppose it was the memories, but suddenly a
few slices of French toast slathered in butter
and coated in syrup sounded quite
delectable.

As I followed Lisa along the curving
highway, I felt the cool mountain breeze
whisk past me. A light mist ascended just
above the trees, and the day felt
invigorating.

213

As much as I yearned for a long night's sleep, one that doesn't usually end till around ten in the morning, I still love the early morning. Everything is vibrant and fresh.

The parking lot of the Red Rooster was already filling with some of Barnes County's early risers. I parked next to Lisa's Mazda.

I walked through the door and nearly froze. I felt like a kid as I marveled at the decorum that had not been altered in ten years. After so many years, one might forget some of the details. I could see them all; from the cheesy painting of a giant rooster hanging over the cash register. The long counter ran along the side wall, and I could, for a moment, see my father sitting there sipping a cup of coffee and poking fun with "Miss Jean."

"Max," Lisa said, and I was jerked from the bygone days. I felt myself exhale again before I looked at her.

"Do you want to sit at the counter?" she

asked.

I looked back at the empty stool. "Why don't we get that table in the corner?"

Lisa nodded and then she navigated the maze around the tables toward the corner. The old men were jibing each other and an occasional cackle would resound from someone's jest. Breakfast was their reprieve for the day. A few moments before the day's work began.

We had seated, and I lifted the laminated menu. The type was newer, and the prices were a bit higher. Otherwise, the food was most likely the same. I looked behind the counter, and Jean Durange was passing a plate of eggs, bacon, and a golden biscuit to an elderly gentleman in faded overalls. Jean Durange may have had a few new wrinkles or a few new white hairs, but she still looked the same to me.

I took another look at the menu. "French toast," I said.

"What?" Lisa asked.

"I think I will have Marty's French toast. He always made the best French toast."

Lisa frowned, "Yeah, but Mr. Durange died a few years ago."

I leaned back with shock.

Lisa answered the question I hadn't had time to ask. "He got lung cancer about three or four years ago. He refused to let Jean close the place. He said he would work until he couldn't stand."

"That's awful. Does Jean run the place alone?"

"Their oldest son, Mike, helps her now. She got some offers to sell, but she refused because it was Marty's place."

"I guess some things do change." I could feel my insides swell, and I fought to retain my composure.

"Morning Lisa." Jean Durange came up behind Lisa.

"Morning, Miss Jean. How are you this morning?"

"Doing well. Everyone is buzzing about these two killings this weekend."

I smiled at the Hellenston news network. Most people probably heard about Mark Lofton on Friday, and Leigh Rozen-Lofton's sudden suicide probably took precedence over whatever Sunday school topics were being preached in the different churches across the county.

"So Lisa, who is your friend?" Jean asked.

"Miss Jean, you remember Max Sawyer, don't you?"

Jean Durange studied me closely. Her eyes examined me up and down. "Ronnie's boy?"

"Yes ma'am," I said.

She smiled a large grin, "Well, I'll be. Haven't you grown up? Well, stand up and give me a hug."

I submitted as she continued to speak, "I haven't seen you in years. How are you doing?"

"I'm good."

"I remember you and your dad used to come in here all the time for breakfast."

"Yes ma'am," I responded.

"Well," she said slowly as she shook her head, "I best get your order. Other folks'll get hungry if I don't get in gear."

"I would love the French toast," I said, "and a cup of coffee."

Jean looked at Lisa, "How about you, hon?"

"Two eggs scrambled, and a slice of toast."

"Want some coffee?"

"Yes ma'am," Lisa answered.

Miss Jean turned and carried our order to the kitchen. Within a minute she had returned with two cups of coffee. I immediately doctored mine with a bit of sugar and a dash of cream. Lisa, however, wasted no time by drinking it black.

"Can I ask you a question?" Lisa prodded.

I lifted my head from my coffee so that my eyes met hers. She glowed with personal curiosity. "I suppose."

"You never come home. Nobody has seen you in over a decade. Why?"

I shrugged, "Why come here? I have no family left here. Besides, I have been back on occasion."

"You missed our ten-year reunion back in May," Lisa said.

"I know, but I didn't think I would be all that welcome. I have a feeling that there are still a few people here who don't care too much for me. And I feel the same towards them."

Lisa batted her eyes and replied, "That's not a healthy attitude to have."

"Thanks for your opinion, Dr. Laura."

Lisa narrowed her gaze at me, "I don't think anyone holds a grudge against you."

"What about Peter Daniels? He didn't seem excited to see me. I am sure you got an earful after I left."

"No, Peter didn't say a word. But he's different."

"So, his brother went to prison on my account, and it's okay for him to begrudge me. I suppose I should forgive all. I mean my folks were only murdered in their sleep."

Lisa's face drooped, "I didn't mean that. Of course, there are going to be those feelings. Most people in this town were relieved when Hanson went to prison. Most folks prayed and cried about you. For years, people wondered about you."

"Nothing to really wonder about. I got on with my life."

"Did you really? You just vanished the day after they sentenced Hanson and Daniels."

"I did get on with my life. I left the past here. I didn't forget it."

Lisa touched my hand, "I'm glad you came back. I'm sure Mandy was happy to see you. Obviously, Miss Jean is, too."

I smiled. Lisa smiled back, and for a

second I didn't want to look away.

"Did I ever tell you that I read all of your articles?" Lisa asked.

"No." I was a bit surprised. I had a degree in journalism and had written for the Memphis paper for about a year. Most of my stuff had been basic police blotter: rape, murder, and burglaries.

"We get most of the major papers from the area. Little Rock, Fayetteville, Memphis. I was just a reporter, but I made it a mission to read every word in every paper. I remember seeing your first piece. I started looking for them after that."

I laughed, "I'm impressed. Unfortunately, none of them were Pulitzer pieces."

"Whose are?" Lisa said.

"Good point."

"You quit?"

"Yeah, I found out I hated journalists."

"Hey," Lisa grinned.

"Present company excluded."

Our conversation halted as our breakfast arrived. I sliced into the golden brown toast. I placed the bite into my mouth, and I let my palette absorb the flavor. It may not have been Marty's French toast, but it was still delicious.

I was about halfway through my toast when I raised my eyes to see Scott Gaither entering through the door. I continued to chew the bite of toast slowly as I peered at him. Gaither immediately noticed me. He gave a half smile before moving toward us.

"Mr. Sawyer," he said as he pulled a chair away from the table and sat down, "do you mind if I join you?"

He nodded to Lisa, "How are you, Lisa?"

"I'm fine, Scott."

"You look hungry, Scott. Why don't you buy us some breakfast?"

Scott smirked, "Fine, I'll treat. You just tell me what the two of you were doing at Ms. Rozen's trailer this morning."

I glanced at Lisa and lifted an eyebrow. She also looked a bit shocked.

"I don't hear any explanations," Scott said gruffly.

"I can assure you," I stated, "that we did not tamper with any evidence."

"You're a smartass!"

"I know," I beamed proudly.

Lisa jumped into the fray saying, "Scott, we were just trying to find anything unusual."

"There is something unusual about two people nosing around a crime scene."

"When did suicide become a crime?" I asked matter-of-factly.

Scott shot me with a look and said, "Shut up, Sawyer."

"Scott..." Lisa started.

"No, Lisa," Scott cut her off, "this man is about to be arrested for obstruction of justice. If you don't have any desire to share a cell with him, then you better stay clear of him."

Scott turned his gaze toward me, "Sawyer, consider yourself lucky. I really have no desire to arrest Lisa here, so I am letting you off this time. If you cross me again, I will throw you in jail."

I took a long sip of coffee and then leaned closer to Sheriff Gaither. "I dare you to arrest me," I whispered, "I'm betting that you couldn't keep me there long."

Scott refused to break his stare as he warned, "Try me."

I took the last bite of my French toast and chewed it slowly. Lisa stared at us fearfully waiting for the next onslaught of verbal assaults. Scott continued to scowl at me.

I laid the fork on the table. I handed the menu to Scott, "Don't you want to order something?"

Scott stood up, "I think I lost my appetite."

"I hope you didn't lose your wallet," I said handing him the check. Scott walked away quickly, and I laid the check back on the table. I finished my coffee while Lisa gawked blankly at me.

I smiled, "He certainly seems happy that I came back."

"Why are you taunting him? He could arrest you."

"He could, but he probably won't. Unless he can make it stick."

Lisa wrinkled her brow, "Don't bet against Scott, he is a pretty good guy."

I shrugged and said, "I am sorry I was rude to him."

Lisa said, "I don't think you really are sorry. I guess that's okay, though."

"You're right, I'm not. Although I am certain that Scott is a good guy."

"What do you plan to do today?" Lisa changed the subject.

"I need to connect Nichols. What do you think you can get?"

"I can see. I could always interview him under the pretense of talking about this case.   This is the biggest murder case ...."

"In a decade." I finished her thought.

"I didn't mean..."

"It's okay," I assured her.

Lisa snatched the check and took a glimpse at it. She pulled a twenty from her purse and dropped it on the table. Miss Jean materialized to take the money.

"Thanks for the breakfast," I said as we walked out of the Red Rooster.

"Do you want to meet me later? We can see if we have gotten any leads."

"Sounds good," I said as I escorted Lisa to her car. "How about lunch?"

"Meet me at the paper about noon. We can find a bite to eat around there."

"See you at noon," I said as she leaned in and placed a small kiss on my cheek.

I opened her door and let her into her car. I stood there and watched as she drove out of the lot. I reached into my pocket and began searching for my keys.

"Hey!" A voice called.

I spun around to see three men beside a blue truck across the lot. My heart stopped for a second as I found myself face to face with Billy Daniels. Billy was Peter Daniels brother who had gone to prison for his involvement in my parent's murder. He had helped Sheriff Hanson attempt to suppress some of the evidence. He had been convicted, and until this moment, I thought he was still in prison.

"Max Sawyer," Daniels sneered, "I heard that you were in town."

I stood silent.

"Don't you think you should be leaving? I'm sure you don't have any pressing business here." Daniels moved closer.

"Billy, you might want to be careful. I'm not a kid anymore, and I don't take too kindly to threats."

"Who's threatening you? I just don't want anything to happen to you. I might be blamed for something I had nothing to do with."

I pride myself on my self-control, but in that instant I became enraged. I leaped forward, and in two steps, I jumped up and kicked Billy Daniels in the stomach.

Billy doubled over with a grunt. His two companions took only half a second to descend upon me. I was mad, fighting quickly to keep them at bay. Suddenly my feet buckled as Billy tackled me from behind.

I hit the ground, and Billy was coming down on me. I winced in anticipation.

"Billy! Stop it, Billy!"

I couldn't see who was shouting, but I was grateful for the breather.

"I was just talking to him," Billy said, "He started it."

I peeked past Billy to see the voice's owner. I was surprised to see Peter Daniels standing there ordering his older brother off of me.

"Billy," Peter said, "they will send you

back in a heartbeat. Just leave him alone."

Billy Daniels frowned at me and scoffed, "Fine, I'm going."

I sat up and watched Billy walk into the Red Rooster. Several of the patrons had exited to watch the commotion. Peter walked over to me and offered his hand. I took hold of it and pulled myself to my feet.

"Sorry about him, Max."

"Thanks, Peter." I brushed myself off and said, "He was right, I hit him first."

Peter shook his head, "If I know my brother, he was asking for it."

"He was," I said, "but thanks again."

"He's still my brother," Peter began, "but I am really sorry for what he has done to you."

I wanted to say something, but I was speechless. I couldn't find the right words, so I stood silently.

"I always looked up to him as a kid. I guess people change."

"Sometimes they do," was all I could

think to say.

"I need to go, Max. I'll see you around."

"See ya, Peter," I said as he walked inside the Red Rooster.

I walked back to my car thinking about what Lisa had said earlier. It was 7:15 a.m., and I was already having an eventful day. I needed a shower and a change of clothes. I wanted to see Tom in order to give him an update on the recent happenings, but he wouldn't be in his office until after eight. I had a little time to get back to the boat and squeeze in a shower.

27

Mandy was still asleep when I left the
boat again. I scrawled a note for her before I
headed to Tom's office. I had showered
quickly as I was in a hurry to talk to Tom.
Despite my rush, I thought I would stop and
grab a couple of jelly doughnuts. Tom was a
connoisseur of jelly doughnuts, so I gave
him a small selection of strawberry,
blueberry,
and raspberry.

I walked into his office at 8:34 a.m.
Mrs. McEwan sat behind her desk staring
into her computer. Her eyes looked over her
glasses as I entered, and her head never
wavered.

"Mr. Sawyer," she said.

"Good morning, Mrs. McEwan."

"I see you are still in town. I assumed by now you would be rock climbing the Amazon."

"I am waiting for you to come along."

Her lips puckered like she had a lemon tight between them. She ignored me and returned immediately to her computer screen.

"I dropped by to talk to Tom," I said.

Mrs. McEwan stopped typing and turned her head. "You didn't just come to see me?"

I was stunned and taken aback by such sarcasm and wit coming from her. I would have been less surprised to hear her curse me. Nonetheless, I couldn't let her get in the last blow. I leaned over her desk and placed a sloppy kiss on her cheek.

"Max," came Tom's voice, "come on back."

"Later," I winked at Mrs. McEwan.

I walked into Tom's office and tossed the bag of jelly doughnuts across the desk.

"What's this?" Tom asked as he tore open the sack like a wild dog.

"A sacrificial offering."

Tom pulled the blueberry doughnut from the bag and said, "Thanks, Max. What are you trying to butter me up for?"

"Nothing," I said, "but I do have a bit of a break that I wanted to talk to you about."

Tom nodded, and I proceeded to relate everything that had transpired since yesterday morning. I started with J.T.'s Club and Lofton's apparent theft. I finished with my return to Leigh Rozen's trailer and my subsequent discovery.

I pulled the cigarette butt from my pocket and laid it gently on his desk.

"What is this?"

"A Dunhill cigarette butt."

"So!" Tom seemed a bit flustered.

"It's an unusual brand. Probably not easy to buy in this town. But it is also the preferred cigarette of Charlie Nichols."

Tom craned his neck forward and said

in a deep, solemn voice, "Are you telling me that Charlie Nichols killed Leigh Rozen?"

"I believe so. Maybe even Mark Lofton."

"This is absurd," Tom said, "Charlie is Amanda Rawls' lawyer. This is purely circumstantial."

"I know, this whole case is very strange."

"Max, stop this. I knew it was a mistake to call you." Tom's glare turned menacing.

"Tom..." I started.

"No, Max," he cut me off, "I don't want you in this. You are going to ruin a man's reputation with your stupid conspiracies and accusations."

"Tom..." I tried to speak again, but he stopped me again.

"Did it occur to you that perhaps the police are right? Maybe Amanda Rawls did kill Mark Lofton. Maybe not. Either way, I want you to stay out of this. If you don't, so help me, I will have you charged with obstruction of justice.

"Now, thank you for the doughnuts, but I have a lot of work to do. I have to see your girlfriend in court tomorrow."

I had never seen Tom this angry about anything. I was unable to speak. I stood silently and shuffled away like the scolded child I was.

28

I was still reeling from the verbal lashing I had just received. I felt like a teenager who just brought home a poor report card. I stood in front of the courthouse shaking with a fear I hadn't felt in years.

For a split second, an urge to leave came over me. I could climb into my car, and in three hours, I could be sitting in my apartment in Memphis.

I walked past my parked car, though. I always feel the need to walk whenever I find myself lost. If I walk long enough, eventually I find where I am.

I passed all the stores on Main Street. Each step seemed to move me into my conundrum. Tom had been like a father to me over the past few years. He was like a brother to my own father. Hell, he was family.

And right now, I was compelled to defy him. I wanted to prove him wrong, or maybe I wanted to show him that I was right.

I knew where I was walking, even if I was taking the long route. So I wasn't surprised to stop in front of the office of Charlie Nichols. I knew exactly where I had been going; what I was going to do was going to be the surprise.

"Mr. Sawyer," Charlie Nichols said as I entered his office, "how are you this morning?"

He was standing next to a file cabinet. His tie was loosened, and his sleeves were rolled back to his elbows. He held a manila file folder in his right hand and the incriminating cigarette in his left. He immediately placed the cigarette between his lips, passed the folder to his left hand, and extended his right hand to greet me.

I shook his hand and said, "I need to talk to you."

"Good, good," his head bobbed, "I want to assure you that Amanda is in good hands. I am absolutely certain we can establish a case with self-defense."

I gently bit the inside of my lip. Tom might have been right. If Charlie Nichols was innocent, then it would have been unfair to make a public accusation. On the other hand, if he did kill Mark and Leigh, then my private accusation might be an incentive to croak me as well.

Oh, well, what is life without risk?

I took the break in his speech to dive into the cesspool. "Did you kill Leigh Rozen?"

"What?" He appeared shocked. I was uncertain if it was a genuine shock. It was hard to tell. He was a lawyer, after all.

I repeated my question, "Did you kill Leigh Rozen? Mark Lofton's wife?"

"I know who she is!" He sat down

behind his desk. "Why would I kill her?"

"I don't know yet. And the appropriate word is 'yet.' Why don't you save me the trouble and tell me why you killed her?"

His nose flared and his cheeks turned a crimson red, "I don't know what you are getting at Sawyer. I had no reason to kill Leigh. As I hear it, you were the only one arrested at her place."

"I was only detained," I replied. "I know why I was there. I am also fairly certain that I didn't kill her."

"Neither did I."

I was beginning to realize that my bluntness was most likely not the shrewdest techniques of questioning. I presumed that he would instantly concede and confess his evil deeds. Once again I was grossly mistaken.

"Mr. Nichols, I found this in her trailer." I laid the Dunhill butt on his desk.

Nichols peered closely at it. He made certain he never touched it.

"It's your brand. It's an unusual brand that I would bet you alone in this town smoke."

His eyes lit up with fear as he whispered, "I didn't kill her."

"What were you doing there, then?" I demanded. I felt smug as I saw myself circling him.

"I wasn't there. I haven't been there in months."

My brow furrowed. He had been there, but I was absolutely confused.

"When were you there?" I asked softer than I had before.

"I finalized Leigh's divorce. I was out there taking her the paperwork a few months back." Nichols' voice was shaky. He wasn't being entirely honest.

"Do you make a lot of house calls?"

"No, on occasion. She..."

"Bartered for your services?"

He nodded, yes.

My head was swimming again. I

believed him. He was distraught and panicking. He could still be capable of killing her.

"Drugs or sex?"

"She said she would sleep with me."

"Okay," I continued, "how long did the two of you have this relationship?"

"Just a few weeks back in June. One more time in July."

"Did you ever go out behind the trailer?" I asked.

"Why would I?" he still sounded sincere and scared.

"Where do you get your smokes?"

"I have to get them in Little Rock. There is a little tobacco shop across from the courthouse I usually go to."

"Know anyone else who smokes Dunhill?"

No, he shook his head.

I stared at him for a moment. He was holding his head with his left hand. He had extinguished his cigarette in the ashtray. I saw the wedding band on his hand, and something in my mind popped. Tom knew about Charlie and Leigh. He knew, or at least he thought, that Charlie didn't kill her. He was concerned about Charlie's reputation. Or was he?

"How does Tom know about this?" I asked.

Charlie Nichols looked at me, "I don't know."

"Mr. Nichols. Charlie, I am sorry if I jumped to the wrong conclusion." I stood up to leave and added, "Don't worry. This isn't going past me. You have my word."

He continued to stare at me, and I couldn't tell if he was grateful or if he wanted to tell me to get out.

I walked out of his office and stormed down Main Street. How did Tom know? Maybe it wasn't important, but Tom went out of the way to make me feel like I was wrong. I had a sick feeling growing in my gut. I walked into Tom's office. Mrs.

McEwan glanced up, but I didn't slow down to parry snide remarks. I walked through Tom's door and pushed it shut.

"Max?"

"You knew about Charlie Nichols!" I sat down opposite Tom's desk.

"Max..."

I cut him off, "Now, I ask myself, 'How did you know about them?' I can only figure two answers to the question. I am pretty sure that he never told you about it."

Tom leaned back in his chair. He held a black pen in his right hand that he began to tap on the edge of his desk. He cleared his throat, and we stared at each other for an instant.

Finally, he spoke, "I did know. Back in February, Cathy left me. It was after our anniversary. Twenty-eight years. She said that I was too wrapped up in everything but her. She was lonely, so she left. She moved in with her sister in Little Rock.

"Four months passed, and she still

hadn't come home. By that time, I figured she might never. I began to get a little down, and one night I stopped at Mike's Bar out Highway 16. I met Leigh there. I had drunk quite a lot with her before she took me back to her place. We, us..."

"I get it, Tom."

"After that, I couldn't even work. I was more miserable, and I realized that there was no one who could take Cathy's place. I drove to Little Rock and begged her to come home. We went to Barbados for three weeks. When we got back, she came home with me."

"Does Cathy know?" I asked.

"Yes."

"And Charlie Nichols?"

"Leigh bragged about being with Charlie. That he did her divorce for free."

I leaned back, "So, you knew Leigh Rozen. You knew Charlie Nichols knew her. You even laid into me about this. You don't think this was important?"

"How is it important? Did I ask about your relationship to Ms. Rawls? It doesn't have a bearing on the case, and frankly, it was none of your business."

"It might. It seems like a good motive for either one of you. Besides we are friends, you must have known I might find out."

"I hoped you wouldn't," whispered Tom.

"Surprise, I did."

Tom sat mute. I examined him. I felt betrayed.

"What can you tell me about Leigh Rozen?" I finally asked.

"She has no record. Nothing criminal. Everything else you have most likely already deduced."

I was a little shocked. I had expected at least a prostitution or possession charge. It was odd to find someone like her who had skirted the police thus far. She was an anomaly.

However, everything about this case appeared to be an anomaly.

I stood to leave and said, "You're an ass! You berated me in order to keep a secret that doesn't even matter. Cathy already knew."

"But Teresa Nichols doesn't know."

"Just so you know," I said, "I am going to find out who did kill Mark and Leigh Lofton."

"I know," he said as I turned to leave the office.

29

I was standing on the sidewalk along Main Street when my phone rang. I quickly answered it.

"Max," said John Woods.

"Hey, John, how's it going?"

"Depends on your point of view," he answered. "I have some news for you."

"Give it to me."

"The number you gave me belongs to a pager. Unfortunately, it's a prepaid deal from one of those hole-in-the-wall stores. The store's called Cell Etc. in North Little Rock on Jackson Avenue."

"Was there a name with it?"

"Nothing legit. The name was Scott Shelby, but the social and address were faked. These places don't care for details as long as you are prepaying."

"Thanks, John. Can I ask one more favor?"

I wanted to check all of the calls to and from Leigh Rozen over the past few months. Especially anything that struck an unusual chord. John agreed to unofficially check.

"I owe you," I said.

"Fine, get up here so you can take me out someplace fancy and liquor me up."

"Deal, but you gotta wear something pretty."

John chuckled into the phone.

I hung up the phone. A pager wasn't much. It could have easily been her drug connection.

I hadn't moved a step when my phone rang again.

"Did you see the news?" Lisa asked.

"No."

"Paul Grace was shot this morning."

"Is he dead?"

"Yeah. The news is saying it was a

drive-by. They imply it was related to his
business."

"I'm sure it was," I said. "Where are
you?"

"At the paper."

"I will be there in ten minutes."

"You just can't get enough of me, huh?"

I laughed and hung up on her.

It was 9:41 a.m. and today was
beginning to look like a long day. A long,
eventful day.

I walked across the square to the paper
in less than ten minutes. Seven, if anyone is
really counting. I didn't have a lot of time to
mull over Grace's death, but I tried to
manage.

Paul Grace could have easily been
killed by some business partner he screwed.
Maybe even some crazy, zealous Christian
who God told to rid the world of its dirty,
old porn dealers. It was even possible that
our killer had struck once more. I wanted to
hold my judgment.

Lisa was sitting behind an old, metal desk that had probably seen more reporters than Madonna, the Pope, and Prince William put together. She had a small television in the corner of her office on one of the Little Rock stations. She was tapping away on her computer as she kept one eye on the news for another report on Grace's murder.

Lisa peeked at me from her computer. I wanted to smile when I saw those bright blue eyes. I don't think I had ever really noticed them. They were blue like the sky. Almost pale, and they shimmered when she smiled.

I quivered as I tried to focus my mind, but I truly reveled in this feeling that I had abruptly overtaken me. I lamented that now was not the time.

"Hear anything yet?" I asked.

"Nothing new."

"We probably won't for now."

Lisa gave a shrug and asked, "Have we learned anything about Nichols?"

"Quite a lot. He denies having been there in months. He apparently finalized her divorce for her back in June." I had promised Charlie that his secret was safe with me, so unless it became relevant, I wasn't going to tell anyone.

"So, he's not our guy?" Lisa asked.

"Not necessarily. I believed him, so his odds have improved. I don't know that I am going to count him out just yet."

"Where does that leave us?" Lisa inquired.

"In the lurch, so to speak."

Lisa gave a little shrug, "Well, it's a little too early for lunch. Do you think we should get to Little Rock to check into Paul Grace's death?"

"I'd bet the Little Rock cops are covering it better than we can. Besides if it was only business related, then we are sure to hear."

Lisa agreed. The question remained, what avenue did we next pursue?

251

"I have an idea," I said, "but it's pretty radical."

"How radical?" Lisa asked.

"Let me say that it is an extreme measure that I don't think you should be forced to witness."

"What is it?" she probed.

"I'm going to ask Scott Gaither for help."

Lisa smiled, "You aren't about to leave me out. I wouldn't miss this for the world."

30

Scott Gaither was sitting behind his desk when we walked into his office. He stopped writing and glanced at us.

"What is it with you two?" He put his pen down on the desk. "I can't go two hours without seeing the two of you."

"I want to talk to you, Scott."

Scott's face contorted with confusion and distrust. He looked to Lisa.

"Don't look at me," Lisa said, "I am just here for the show."

"Great," was Scott's response.

Lisa stood in the doorway and leaned against the frame. I sat down opposite Scott. His face was dripping with suspicion.

"I want to lay my cards on the table," I began. "Lisa has been attesting to your character, so I want to apologize if I have acted or treated you unfairly."

Scott's demeanor had obviously been stunned. He stared ahead in disbelief.

I continued, "I need your help. I...well, Lisa and I have done a bit of digging, but we have hit a few walls. So I had hoped that we could pool our resources."

"I see," Scott replied. "What is it I can do for you?"

"I just wanted to see that someone more official had the details we have uncovered, should something happen."

Scott nodded warily, "Okay, Sawyer, spill it."

And spill it, I did. I gave Scott a fairly detailed run down of everything that Lisa and I knew so far. Several times throughout my tale, Scott would interrupt to state that a particular piece of information was already a known fact. I wanted to smile, but instead I continued with the facts. The only tidbit that I forgot to tell Scott was Charlie Nichols unofficial involvement with Leigh Rozen. I only hoped that Lisa wouldn't speak up unexpectedly. She didn't. Scott absorbed it all. He tried not to show surprise about Paul Grace's connection. While I was sure that Scott had discovered Mark Lofton's unusual bank activity, he had, but I also was sure, not known the source of the money.

"That's pretty interesting," Scott commented. "What do you want from me?"

"All I really want is your assurance that Mandy Rawls is given fair treatment. That you will help me prove that she is innocent."

"Look, Max, I always liked Mandy. I didn't enjoy arresting her. I can even understand why she did it considering the circumstances. Unfortunately, she was standing over the body with the murder weapon at hand. She is the best suspect I have seen."

"Will you be looking into any other suspects now?"

"Given what you have told me, I can

assure you that I will."

I smiled, "That's all I wanted in the first place."

Scott carried a pensive countenance, "Thanks a lot, Max."

"I do have one question, though. Perhaps you can help." I was ready to strike. Then I shot the question, "Did you ever trace the numbers that called in both murders?"

"I don't have anything on it," Scott said solemnly.

"C'mon Scott. I am sure you ran a check on the phone records. I was just curious if it was the same number. I was wondering if the number might be traced back to Cell Etc. or some other prepaid service."

Scott remained still. Then he said slowly, "I appreciate the details that you have given me, but I just can't share information from an active investigation. Sorry, Max."

"Don't sweat it. Thanks anyhow. I am

sure that Mandy's attorney will be able to find out if it might help her."

"Probably so," Scott said.

I nodded and stood up. I offered my hand to Scott. He hesitated for a second, but then he shook it firmly. I was certain he was a bit confused by my sudden change of heart.

However, he was still quite friendlier than he had been. I knew that he didn't trust me. That was exactly what I wanted from him.

Scott warned me and Lisa about snooping around in his investigation. I simply promised to stay out of his way. He seemed content, but I knew he would be watching.

31

"Now what?" Lisa asked.

"Lunch. Then maybe some fishing?"

Lisa stopped on the sidewalk in front of the sheriff office. Her face twisted in confusion.

"Excuse me?" she asked.

"We relax. I think we have hit a wall until something comes up, so we eat a nice lunch. Then you will probably go back to work unless I can talk you into going fishing with me."

"Alright," she said with exasperation, "I'm lost. Are we quitting?"

"No, in fact, I only know of a few small things we can check. So unless something big comes up we can take the rest of the day off."

"Something big? What just happened inside there?"

"Think about it. Do we have any leads?"

Lisa thought about it, "Sure we could find Jeff Thomas and ask him a few questions. See what he knows."

"Jeff Thomas is a thug. He might be too dumb to not kill us. Besides Scott should be able to track some of the money to him. The police will have better luck with him than we would."

"Are you trying to ditch me?" she asked.

"Not at all. I want to go fishing. I was thinking about finding John Mead to see if he could shed any light on Lofton."

"You are planning on ditching me, aren't you?"

"No, can you leave now? Or do you have some work to do?"

"I can shuffle some papers around and be through in about half an hour."

"Fine, let me go find John Mead. I will be back in half an hour to pick you up."

"You're buying lunch, right?" she asked.

"Of course."

Lisa finally accepted my offer.

"Great," I exclaimed, "I need someone to bait my hook. Worms make me squeamish."

Lisa laughed loudly.

32

While Lisa finished her work, I jumped on the horn to track down John Mead. I wanted to know about Lofton away from Mandy. Construction sites often lead to people bragging about different things. Everyone has to top the other guy's tale, and if one guy has a girl, then the next needs to have two. Lofton may have let some secrets out during a bragging session.

I called Mead's office, and his secretary informed me that he was out in Chimney Rock working. Chimney Rock was a small isle in a wide patch of the river. It housed several of the most expensive homes in Barnes County. Many weekenders from Memphis or Little Rock kept nice houses there. My parents' house was still there, sitting vacant.

I took down the address and headed toward home. From downtown Hellenston, I could make the route to Chimney Rock in about 15 minutes. I did make the trip once in less than eight minutes. I had left Beth Horton's house with nine minutes to get in before my curfew. Beth had a beautiful set of blue eyes with a slightly purple hue and curly red hair. Not red like Charlie Brown's little girlfriend, but a soft auburn color. Her hair always kinked up when it was wet or the humidity skyrocketed. She liked to write poetry. Bad poetry that was usually about love or birds, or occasionally lovebirds. I wondered how she was doing.

I found the address and parked in front of the house. There were two white trucks in the drive. Both looked like typical construction trucks, loaded with building supplies and scraps. I walked around the house and through a gate leading into the backyard. I could see the addition being built on the house.

Two men were sitting on a knoll on the ground and working on what appeared to be sack lunches.

One was an older man in his 50's. His hair was thinning and graying. He wore a white t-shirt that was sprinkled with sawdust. A plaid button down shirt was lying across a sawhorse. The younger guy was in his early 20's. His hair was buzzed to almost nothing. He wore a maroon t-shirt with a Razorback on steroids bursting through a wall.

He held a sandwich in one hand and a cigarette between his lips. He would alternate the cigarette and the sandwich to his mouth.

"Mr. Mead?" I asked.

"Yes," the older man spoke cautiously.

"Mr. Mead, I'm Max Sawyer. I just wanted to talk to you for a minute."

Mead put his sandwich into the bag, "'Bout what?"

I sat down on the ground near him, "Please go ahead and eat. I just wanted to know a little about Mark Lofton."

"Mark? Are you a reporter or something?"

"Something. I am trying to find out why he got killed."

Mead looked at the younger guy who shrugged. "Okay," he said, "Mark was a good kid."

"I understand that he worked for you."

"Yeah," Mead answered, "he worked for me for over two years."

"Then he just stopped showing up to work?"

Mead shook his head, "No. He came to me a few months back. Said his girlfriend got him a job in Little Rock. Supposed to be making a lot of money. Anyway, he wanted to know if I could use him on occasion when he wasn't working there. He was a good worker, so I told him I could."

"Did he say what the job in Little Rock

was?"

Mead shook his head, but the other guy spoke up, "He said he was going to retire."

"Did Mark get high?"

Both men shook their heads, and Mead said, "Not that I know."

"Did he ever talk about his new wife?"

Mead shook his head, "No, I heard about it. I was a little shocked. He certainly had it in deep for that Rawls girl. Then to up and change so quickly. He never even mentioned it. Probably why she killed him."

I nodded. I was reminded of a wedding that I attended with Nikki a few years ago. The groom had not even wanted a bachelor party, but the bride insisted. The groom had his party, and then he left town with the stripper. The bride called the wedding off with everyone already in the chapel. I was sitting next to a black lady that had worked with the bride. She said it all, "One good freak'll make you crazy."

I thanked them for their time and made

my way back to the car. I began to wonder about Mark. If Leigh had gotten him a job a few months ago, then they knew each other before he began working at J.T.'s Club. How long had he known her? How did they meet?

Maybe everyone was right. Maybe he got exactly what he deserved.

I drove out of Chimney Rock without ever passing the house at 1120 Riverbed Cove. It was another memory I hadn't touched in a decade. I was certain that Tom was keeping the yard and house clean and kept. It had been rented a few times over the years, but now it remained empty.

Lisa was waiting for me when I pulled up to the curb. She jumped into the car and smiled.

"I'm ready to go fishing."

"We aren't going fishing," I said.

"What?" Lisa was surprised.

"We were never going fishing. I found a different angle. So wouldn't you rather do exactly what Scott Gaither told us not to do.?"

"What do you have in mind?"

"Did Mark Lofton have a close friend?" I asked.

"I don't know."

"How about his parents?"

"They live over in Morton," she said.

Morton was a small town with about 62 people. It consisted of one convenience store that boasted that it sold everything from live bait to fine art, depending on one's definition of fine art. Everyone knew Morton because just outside the town was one of the areas little secrets, a cave mouth that lead deep into a dark labyrinth of caverns. Morton's constable had always tried to run kids away from the cave but to no avail. The area was fenced, but again the persistence of teenagers prevailed. Nearly every high school students from anywhere nearby had spent the night in the caves with a six pack or a bag of weed. Only two kids ever got

267

lost in the caves. Apparently going deeper into the earth until they were never able to get out. That prompted a rush to seal the caverns for good, luckily the landowner refused and the ruckus soon was forgotten.

I looked at Lisa and smiled, "Let's go to Morton."

Lisa tilted her head, "Don't forget that you are still buying me lunch."

"I think I could swing a Big Mac for you."

33

We snagged a couple of burgers from McDonald's before I aimed the Z3 to the north. We were only on the road for five minutes when I noticed a police cruiser on the horizon behind me. I knew Scott would be watching, and he was wasting no time at all. Of course, he was distrustful of me; I was doing exactly what he told me not to do. I sped up to the speed limit, and the cruiser was still behind me.

Whoever got the duty to drive behind me today was going to be in for a long drive. I suppose, though, he could have a worse duty today. It was a beautiful day to be tooling down the highway.

I pushed the remote on the CD changer, and Frank Sinatra began crooning "Fly Me to the Moon." Lisa rolled her head toward me.

"You really listen to this kind of music?" she asked.

"Are you kidding?" I replied, "This is timeless music."

"It's okay."

I smirked and snipped, "I know it's no country ballad, but it makes me feel good."

Lisa listened for a minute. "I might be able to get used to this," she said with a grin.

I downshifted into a curve as Frank pleaded to see what June is like on Jupiter or Mars. My friend continued to stay behind me. Since I had decided to give the officer a nice day, Lisa and I made a concerted effort to stop at any and every possible roadside attraction. I never knew how much one might have to pay for a piece of dead wood carved into an alligator.

By the time we reached Morton, our 45-minute drive had more than doubled. Not surprising, the cruiser was still behind us. I wondered what Scott had said after the officer called in for each stop we made. Lisa gave me the address, and after a few minutes, we found the dirt road that leads to the house. The Lofton's lived in a house that looked like it was encased in plaster. The whole house was a cube. The front yard had no grass after having been parked on by no telling how many run down vehicles.

I couldn't see the police cruiser any longer, but I had a feeling that he hadn't gone far. I parked in the gravel drive.

Lisa got out of the Z3 and looked at the house sadly, "How do...What do you plan to say?"

"The truth. I want to know about Mark and Leigh's relationship."

"Do you think they can help?"

"Let's see."

We walked up to the front door. I felt my heart skip. I felt nervous about talking to these grieving parents. But someone had to speak with them. Perhaps I should have brought Mandy along, but then again that might be a bad idea. She was accused of killing their son.

Mrs. Lofton answered the door. She was in her mid-fifties, and she looked as if she had lived too long in this tiny town. Her visage wore the wear and tear of years of rural family life. Most people don't realize how difficult it is living so far from a real city. Money is rarely abundant, and scrimping becomes a way of life.

"Mrs. Lofton?" I asked.

"Yes," she spoke cautiously.

"My name is Max Sawyer. This is Lisa Day. We are working to bring your son's killer to justice. Can we talk to you?"

"Are you with the police?" she asked.

"We are working with them," I lied. "Ms. Day is with the Barnes County News."

Mrs. Lofton's expression never changed. She was apprehensive and distrustful.

Lisa spoke up, "Mrs. Lofton, I know

it's been hard for you. We only have a few questions we need answers to. Hopefully, we can find and help convict his murderer. If it's too hard, we understand.

Lisa was articulate and an artist. Mrs. Lofton's eyes soothed and she pushed the door open for us to enter.

"I thought they arrested Mandy for killing him?" she asked as we walked through the door.

We entered the Lofton's living room. There was an orange couch with wooden armrests and a paisley pattern that was quite loud. Two identical gray Laz-E-Boy recliners were situated around an old console television in the corner. The room was sprinkled with cheap ceramic pieces that looked like they had been purchased at flea markets or yard sales. The room was lined with the fake wood paneling that had been quite popular in the late 70's and early 80's.

On the wall were some assorted family

pictures, including a picture of Mandy and Mark, took near a lake. They looked very happy in the picture, and it seemed strange to consider what was flowing underneath.

On the opposite wall was one of the Magic Eye pictures that were popular about twelve years ago. The idea was that if you stared at this montage of tiny photos then eventually a larger image would appear to pop out of the picture. I looked at it for a moment, and a tiger head protruded through the chaotic images.

Mrs. Lofton rested in one of the gray recliners. Lisa and I sat on the orange couch.

"Yes, ma'am," I answered her, "The police have arrested Amanda Rawls, but we are curious if you think she was capable of killing him."

Mrs. Lofton looked off at the picture of Mark and Mandy. "I don't know," she said softly.

"How did Mark feel about Mandy?" I asked.

"He always seemed to love her. They came here every Sunday for lunch. He doted on her and she acted like she loved him."

"What about Leigh Rozen? How did he feel about her?"

Mrs. Lofton shook her head, "He never told us about her. We didn't even know he was married until Friday. Everything seemed fine the last time we saw Mark and Mandy.

"When was that?" Lisa asked.

"About two weeks ago. Mark called and said that they wouldn't make it last Sunday."

"Do you think Mark had been seeing Ms. Rozen before that?" I asked.

She was tearing up, "I don't know. I didn't know him at all."

Lisa moved closer to comfort her, and Mrs. Lofton continued to talk,

"Poor Mandy must have been heartbroken. I don't know what came over him."

A good freak, I thought to myself.

Mrs. Lofton grieved for a few minutes with Lisa holding her hand. I sat quietly and let some things mull around in my head. Lisa continued to console her, and eventually she gave Mrs. Lofton her number in case she needed to talk.

We left after Mrs. Lofton had stopped crying. I was only on the highway for a minute before I reacquired our stalking cruiser. He had obviously been waiting for us to leave the Lofton's home.

Lisa appeared to be relieved to get out of the house. She brushed back her hair and let it flow through the wind. She leaned her head back.

"What did we learn?" she asked.

"Nothing new, except that Mark Lofton had been seeing Leigh Rozen for some time with some extreme secrecy."

"He was cheating on his fiancé."

"But no one even knew he had gotten

married. There had to be someone who knew he got married."

"Like the preacher?" Lisa asked.

I smiled and looked at her with her soft, brown hair dancing in the wind. "You are brilliant."

"Why thank you," she said with an illuminating smile.

I gunned the engine, shifted up to fifth gear, and aimed the car along the double lines weaving between the mountains.

"Where to now?" she asked.

"I'm going to drop you at the courthouse. We need a copy of the marriage license. Someone married them."

"Better yet," Lisa said, "give me your phone."

I obeyed, and Lisa dialed the number. Within minutes she hung up the phone.

She winked at me, "Steve Reynolds is listed as the officiator."

"Who is he?" I asked.

Lisa shrugged in ignorance.

Lisa made a number of calls, but Steve Reynolds remained in the wind. There were seven Steve Reynolds that lived in the Little Rock area.

"Where was the wedding?" I asked Lisa.

"The license says Little Rock."

"Then let us assume that our Steve Reynolds lives in Little Rock.

That's only seven to shuffle through. Hopefully one is going to be our preacher."

"Do we just start calling?" Lisa asked.

"Might as well," I answered, "put on your best journalist face and start asking questions."

Lisa looked through the numbers and started dialing. Each time she began with a story about being with the state clerk's office. She told them she needed more information concerning a wedding he had performed.

The first four calls insisted that she had the wrong number. The fifth call produced a neurotic voice insisting that he did nothing wrong before abruptly hanging up.

"I think we have a winner," Lisa said with a smile.

"Great," I took the phone from her, "we need to get to him."

"I think he got spooked."

I quickly scanned through the contacts on my phone until I found Austin's number. I pushed the green Talk button. The phone rang.

When Austin answered, I gave him a quick summary and explained what I wanted to get from Steve Reynolds about Mark and Leigh Lofton's nuptials.

"Let me see if I can talk to him," Austin said.

"Great, he seemed spooked so watch yourself," I warned.

He took Steve Reynolds address and number and vowed to call back once he found the guy.

The clock on the dash read 4:27 p.m. I

wanted to talk with Mandy about a few things. I didn't really want Lisa around with Mandy when I talked to her. Up until now, she may not have been aware of how long Lofton had been cheating on her. I was afraid that she may be in for some surprises.

34

It was 6:15 p.m. when I finally got back to the boat. I walked up the gangplank. Mandy was not in the cabin. I climbed up to the top deck to find her sitting in a deck chair.

"Where have you been?" she asked in an almost wifely tone.

"All over," I said in defense, "I think I may be closer to getting you off the hook."

"Really," she exclaimed.

"I have been busy tracking down clues for the past 14 hours."

"What have you found out?" she asked.

I sat down next to Mandy, "It seems Mark may have been stringing you along for longer than you originally thought. He must have been seeing Leigh for a few months.

He kept a lot of people out of the loop. He was leading a very secretive, double life."

Mandy took this news with a good stride. At this point, very little would probably affect her. I assured her that I had every confidence that she would soon be cleared.

After we talked, I decided to prepare my famous shrimp Alfredo. I found a bottle of Deloach Chardonnay, a decent, but inexpensive wine, in the wine cooler.

As we ate, Mandy acted relieved that her ordeal might soon conclude. She ate and drank heartily. Of course, it could have been that my shrimp Alfredo was irresistible.

"We talked to Mark's mother today," I commented when my mouth was available between a thick juicy shrimp and a sip of wine.

"How's Janet doing?" Mandy asked.

It struck me that I had not known Mrs. Lofton's first name. I never thought to ask. I was slightly annoyed at myself for lacking the insight to inquire deeper. I wondered what else I might have overlooked.

"She's not doing too well. She's very confused about Mark," I answered her, "but she said she felt sorry for you."

"She's a nice lady," she said thoughtfully. Then she looked up at me and asked, "What do you mean 'we.'"

I had intentionally left out Lisa from the details. Not that I had any good reasons, I just omitted her involvement. I suppose I had a reason, but I'm sure, in hindsight, that it was a stupid reason. I decided to come clean with Mandy. Eventually, Mandy would have found out that Lisa had been helping.

"I've had some help over the last two days. Lisa Day thinks you are innocent too. She and I have been scurrying about gathering clues."

"Lisa Day?" she furrowed her brow, "I guess it's nice to still have friends."

"It was her idea to find the person that

married Mark and Leigh.

Maybe we can get more details about their relationship."

"That's nice," Mandy said as she downed the last of her glass of chardonnay. She reached for the bottle and filled her glass again.

She slid closer to me and whispered, "I want to thank you, Max. You have gone out of your way to help me."

"Anytime honey. I've always said I would be there for you."

"Lots of folks say that," she whispered before leaning toward me and kissing me softly on the lips. I started to pull back when she kissed me again. Her lips were soft and sweet from the wine. I kissed her back as she slid onto my lap.

For a brief moment, I was sixteen, and this was our first kiss. My pulse quickened with excitement as my arms wound around her. Her hands climbed my back and slid through my hair.

With my eyes closed, I inhaled everything around Mandy. She slipped her hands down my neck and over my chest. I felt her loosen the top button on my shirt. It was followed quickly by a second and a third.

A little voice inside my head kept screaming for me to slow down. I remembered the words of Saint Augustine, "Lord, give me chastity - but not yet."

I am often amazed how little choice sometimes has to do with the final outcome. I made my choice, and it was probably not the wisest of choices. I made my choice quickly, and I was most definitely listening to the voice of Saint Augustine.

But instead chance moved in to alter my choice. The voices in my pants were suddenly joined by a chorus. The chorus turned out to be the ringing of my cell phone from my pants pocket. The initial ring caused everything, including my heart, to freeze. Mandy looked at me with eyes pleading me to not answer its ring.

"It might be important," I said as I tried to pull it free.

It was Austin calling to tell me that he had found our elusive Steve Reynolds.

"Wanna meet me for a drink?" Austin asked.

"Where are you?"

"I'll be in Hellenston in about twenty minutes."

I looked at Mandy, who had loosened the top two buttons of her own shirt. A green bra peeked from beneath, and I was feeling the waves of temptation pounding into me.

"Can we get a rain check? Until I get back, at least?" I was almost ready to beg. "Austin may have found someone to tie the puzzle together."

She slid her hand down my chest, and I was compelled to tell Austin to wait until tomorrow. I made a decision, albeit not a very strong one, to meet Austin. The voice in my head had apparently won out over its southern foe. I was sure though that I would hear some complaints later from down south.

I agreed to meet Austin in half an hour at Berry's, a local tavern. I pulled myself away from a beautiful woman who obviously wanted to have sex with me. I don't know what had come over me. It just seemed unnatural. I might be breaking some unwritten rule. After tonight, I might have to write it down.

I felt a mixture of ecstasy, relief, and regret as I climbed into the car. I skipped through the CD changer until the voice of Billie Holiday brought my car alive. Billie sang to me about how it was "a nice job if you can get it."

"If you can get it, won't you tell me how" I sang along.

35

I let the top down on the BMW. The stars glistened above me as I pulled out of the parking lot of the Prior's Bay Marina. The moon began to peer over the trees as I jetted along the highway. The evening air was cool as I rushed through the night.

I considered calling Lisa, but I felt a bit guilty. I also decided I needed to steer clear of women for at least an hour. I can't stay away much longer from women or I would begin to experience some serious DT's.

I had a lot on my mind. Some things were knotted and tangled so that I could make neither heads nor tails of them. Mark Lofton had clearly been playing with fire. He had stolen some money, a good deal of money, from a local gangster. However,

Paul Grace was dead now. He was a plausible suspect, but the elaborate set-up doesn't seem very Mafioso. Not that I had any idea what actually was Mafioso.

Still, everything looked like it was set up. Mark Lofton had been at Mandy's house for a reason. He might have been there to simply see Mandy, or perhaps he had hidden the money, or at least some of it, there. It would be the least obvious. Mandy would want nothing to do with Mark after he dumped her for Leigh Rozen. He could have hidden the money there without her knowing, and then he could come back for it later. He probably knew the house as well, or at least well enough, to stash something there that Mandy might not find in the near future.

Perhaps his new wife followed him there, or even tagged along. She could have done Mark in and then taken the money. Leaving Mandy to hold the bag might have been the extra poetic justice Leigh would want.

Maybe Leigh had played Mark all along before she killed him. Then her death could have simply been Paul Grace or Jeff Thomas settling the score for good.

I pulled into the parking lot in front of Berry's. Berry's had changed names few times since I was a kid, but the bar had continued to numb the populace of Hellenston for years. It was a cross between a bar and a stable. The back of the bar had a dirt floor for local two-steppers to cut a rug, or perhaps I should say kick up some dust. On the front of the building was a large painted sign next to the front door boasting a Pabst logo.

Something clicked in my head. Jeff Thomas seemed an extremely likely candidate. He might have been able to manipulate Leigh and then kill her. He could have even killed Paul Grace to buy some time. If Jeff Thomas had the missing money then he was certain to be on the first plane to the least extraditable country in the western hemisphere.

I parked the BMW to the side near a red Ford Ranger. I put the top back up and secured it before I got out.

I began to walk toward the entrance when a figure stepped out from behind an old Chevrolet Blazer just to my left. I felt a vibe of trouble shimmy up my spine like a bear up a tree. I turned my head slowly to see Billy Daniels scowling at me. I glanced around to see if his friends were tagging along. They were nowhere to be seen.

"Ain't this a treat," Billy moved closer. "Sawyer, you came along at just the right time."

I looked around the lot. The music from inside the bar filtered outside, but there was not another soul in the parking lot.

I nodded to Billy, "You're right. There's no one here to see you take a beating."

"You think you are so smart," he sneered.

Douglas Pratt

"Billy, Billy, Billy...It's not about how smart I am; it's about how stupid you are."

"Boy, I think you might want to leave. This is my bar."

I shook my head, "Billy, I thought you might have learned a few things. I guess the only thing they taught you inside was how to hold your ankles."

Billy growled and moved in to strike. I took a deep breath and tried to focus. It took at least a second for Billy to throw a punch. It was a slow-moving swing that I blocked and followed with a quick jab to his nose.

Billy stumbled back, and I quickly stepped forward and repeated the jab to his nose. Billy spun away and shook his head. Blood slung from his face. He weaved toward me and charged.

I side stepped him and tagged him on his left cheek with a thrust from my right fist. He wavered as he struggled to keep his balance. I dropped my weight onto my right foot as my left foot rocketed into his gut. He grunted and collapsed to the ground.

I walked around him like a shark around a wounded seal. I wanted to kick him again, but I slowed the rage pounding through my heart.

Billy moved as he tried to get back to his feet. I knelt down and pushed him back to the ground.

"Boy," I said, "I think you might want to leave. This is now my bar."

Blood had pooled underneath his face. He looked up at me and released a spattering of curses.

I smiled and pointed to his nose, "I think you might be bleeding."

He spat at me, and I stood up and walked away.

"Sawyer," he gurgled through the blood dripping down his face, "I swear..."

I didn't care anymore. I kept walking toward the entrance of the bar. I saw Austin standing next to the door.

"I was waiting to see if you needed any

assistance," Austin quipped.

"It was only a small domestic spat," I remarked.

"Yeah, I saw it."

I smiled, "It was just a little problem I have been having since I came into town."

Austin shook my hand, "Looks like you need a beer."

"No, I need a shot of whiskey. Actually about six shots of whiskey."

We walked into the bar. The inside was anything but elegant. There was a long bar with some dingy mirrors and nearly a twenty different neon beer signs illuminating the room with a reddish glow. There was an old jukebox in the corner and a pool table to the side with a group of locals surrounding it. Almost every one of them was wearing a cowboy hat. The bar was fairly busy for a Monday night.

We found a couple of stools at the bar, and the bartender ambled over to us. He was in his early fifties, and he had obviously been doing this kind of work for too long. His face wore deep wrinkles, no doubt from years of late hours and imbibing his own products. He wore a shirt touting Skyy Vodka in addition to a variety of beer stains.

"What can I get you two?" he asked.

"I'll take a Bud Lite," Austin blurted.

The bartender looked at me. "Maker's Mark, please," I said.

"How do you want that?" he asked me.

"Straight, in a shot glass. In fact, bring three. It will save you a couple of trips."

Austin looked at me, "You looking to do some damage?"

"No, that should just about get me started."

The bartender quickly returned with the beer and three shots. I paid him for the round and left a generous tip.

"Thank you," he said when he saw my tip. I lifted one of the shots to him before pouring it down my throat. Austin, likewise, guzzled his beer.

"Steve Reynolds," I said, "You found him?"

Austin swallowed his beer, "Yeah, he was a bit of a squirrel. Seems he met Mark through the strip club. He was a regular, and apparently he had sent off to this online church to become an ordained minister."

I nodded as he continued, "He told me that Mark had approached him and wanted a very discreet wedding."

I slugged the second shot and asked, "Why was he so skittish on the phone?"

"He said that he was afraid that it had been illegal. That the girl on the phone was with the state. Who was the girl?"

I smiled, "Lisa Day has involved herself with me and this murder. She was pulling the state clerk routine to see who would bite."

"Lisa, huh? Yeah, she runs the paper here."

"She's pretty quick too."

Austin looked off toward the jukebox

that was belting out some Alan Jackson tune. He took a long drink and finished his bottle of beer. I gulped my last shot of bourbon.

"Did Steve Reynolds know anything about mark and Leigh's relationship?" I asked.

"No, he said he never even met Leigh Rozen until the ceremony."

"Great," I sighed, "that doesn't help either."

I turned to the bartender and ordered another round for us. He returned twice as quickly with our order. I paid and tipped him again.

"Who do you think did it?" Austin asked.

"I don't know. I think I have enough circumstantial evidence that

Mandy might get acquitted, but I don't have anything hard."

"Did you hear about Paul Grace?" Austin asked.

I nodded and said, "Yeah, it was awfully convenient. I'm not sure, though. He was involved with who knows. His was a dangerous business."

I had reached into my pocket and began fiddling with my lighter on the bar. Austin turned his beer up and was quickly draining it. I followed suit and quickly slammed down the first two shots.

"I don't know what Mark was doing there, though. At Mandy's house."

"Mark was a piece of work," Austin sighed, "I never really liked him. Didn't trust him very much."

"Really, did you tell Mandy about it?"

"Yeah, but I just felt like he was always up to something. I had the feeling like he was trying too hard. I guess it's just hard to explain."

I listened for a minute before I replied. "It just feels staged. The whole murder feels staged to point at Mandy. Like someone lined all the dominoes up and let them lead to Mandy."

"True," Austin said, "if Mandy didn't let him in how did he get there. Wasn't he naked? That doesn't make much sense either."

"No, Mandy said that he was already there and dead when she got there. Either the killer stripped him after he was shot, which is doubtful, or the killer got him to strip and then killed him."

"Where were his clothes?" Austin asked.

"I don't know."

"We should find out how they were found. It would show his state of mind."

I was struck by his epiphany, "So, if they were just thrown about then it might have been a moment of passion."

"Exactly."

Austin brought up a valid point. I would have to research it tomorrow. We talked about a few more things of very little importance. We finished our drinks and decided to call it a night. Austin agreed to meet Mandy and me at the courthouse in the morning.

36

By 10:15 p.m., I had safely made it back to the boat. I wondered if Mandy had already fallen asleep. I boarded my floating abode to find Mandy not asleep. She was, however, waiting in bed for me wearing pretty much just the bed sheet.

Apparently, six shots of Makers Mark had distracted my conscience's voice. I was bombarded with numerous thoughts, some totally incoherent, and some way too clear.

Her eyes told me that she had been waiting for me, which seemed pretty obvious since I was the only one living here. I moved toward the bed with slightly more trepidation than when I had faced Billy Daniels earlier. Naked women tend to throw my focus for a loop, and when she slid the sheet past her breasts and reached for me I could have sworn that I blacked out.

I didn't actually black out, but once I had fallen asleep, I was completely out. I think I was as unconscious as was humanly possible before being comatose. Whether it was the lack of sleep the night before, the six shots of bourbon, or the strenuous workout I just received, I am not sure, but I slept like a rock.

Morning broke much earlier than I would have liked, but I still awoke refreshed. Mandy lay next to me. The sun glistened through the blinds leaving a pattern of lines on her nude back. Her brown hair was ruffled, and the blonde highlights shimmered like gold in the sun.

I decided to slip into the shower. The clock read 6:45 a.m. I could shower and dress before getting Mandy up to go to Charlie Nichols' office.

Mandy didn't have to be in court until 9 a.m., and I wanted Charlie to have all the facts that I had before he went into the courtroom. Perhaps, I hoped, he could get a quick dismissal.

I got into the shower and let the warm water wash over me. I soaped up and rinsed myself quickly. I shut the water off, and the small bathroom was filled with steam. I toweled myself dry and walked out of the bathroom.

Mandy was already awake and dressing. She put on a conservative black suit that I had gotten from her place. She didn't seem nervous about another day in court. Hopefully, I had put some fears to rest with some of the clues I had found.

I dressed in black Kenneth Cole shirt with French cuffs and black Ralph Lauren pants. I put on some gold cufflinks and a pair of black Rockports. I grabbed my phone and my handy pocket tools.

Mandy was ready to go. She started out the door, and I was about to follow. I saw my gun lying on the table. I opted to leave it there since I might be going to the courthouse.

It was almost 7:30 a.m. when we left the marina. We had barely spoken to each other this morning, and outside of a quick kiss when I got out of the shower, one might not have known that we had spent the night together.

The drive, like the rest of the morning, was quiet. Mandy stared off into an abyss that I could only assume were the dreaded thoughts of "what-ifs." It only took ten minutes to get to Main Street. I found a safe parking spot at least 20 feet from anything that might give Scott's boys a chance to ticket me.

"You okay?" I asked.

"Yeah," she said with a half smile, "just nervous."

"Don't worry this is merely a preliminary hearing. Hopefully, the information I've got will help Charlie to get the whole thing dismissed. Don't hold your breath just yet. Everything I've got is circumstantial, but we might still be able to find something concrete."

"Thanks, Max."

"Mandy, we do need to figure out what Mark was doing at your place."

"I don't know. I just don't know."

I touched her hand, "Don't worry. Now, if we suppose that he was there to retrieve the money, where do you think he might have hidden it?"

"I don't know," she almost whimpered, "there are a lot of places to hide something. But I think I would have found it. Besides, why would he hide it at my house?"

"He might have needed someplace that no one would know about."

"The old shack," she said.

"The old shack?"

"Remember, the one back up the mountain."

I did remember the old shack. It was an ancient run down mountain shack about a mile from Mandy's house. It had been a great spot, it was extremely secluded. It seemed like a long hike to stash the money, but if there was a lot of money that needed to be hidden, it might make a good place.

Mandy added, "Mark and I used to hike up there a lot."

I nodded, "Let's go inside. I may go check it out once I leave you with Charlie."

We walked into Charlie's office. Charlie was sitting behind his desk looking more nervous than Mandy. I tried to smile, but he was almost trembling.

"How are you?" I asked slowly.

"Fine," he said curtly.

I looked at Mandy and said, "Could you give me a minute, Mandy?" She had a curious look, but she agreed and stepped into the other office. I waited until she shut the door. I looked over at Charlie

Nichols who looked like he was waiting for the ax to fall.

"Charlie, I am sorry about yesterday. I

was a bit...abrupt, but I am determined to keep what we said between us."

"Thank you, Mr. Sawyer."

"Max," I said. "I had already spoken with Tom before I talked with you. After our conversation yesterday, I went back to him, and he won't spill a word of it."

Charlie nodded with some assurance. Anyone who knew Tom knew that his word was as good as gold.

"Now, I have discovered some interesting details that might well help this case."

Charlie, who seemed to have calmed down, said, "Really, such as?"

I walked over to the other office and told Mandy that she could come back. Once she and I had seated ourselves opposite Charlie, I started.

"There are still a few details that I don't have, and Mandy is still a bit foggy about a few."

"What have you got?" Charlie was

interested.

I described in detail the events of the past few days beginning with Mark Lofton's career at J.T.'s Club and his unusual and fast nuptials. I finished with the details of the stolen money that amounted to an unknown figure.

"What evidence do you have?" Charlie asked.

"None, really. Everything is circumstantial."

Charlie smiled, "That's okay. If we can use it to provide a shred of doubt then we are home free for an acquittal or a mistrial. However, something harder might encourage a dismissal."

Mandy smiled, and I replied, "I'm working on it."

"Don't worry," he said to Mandy, "this is very good news. Do we have any corroborating witnesses?"

I gave him brief details about Lisa, Trouble, Mark Lofton's mother, and Steve

Reynolds, "the minister" for Mark and Leigh. "None of them has anything concrete, but they add to the strangeness behind the sudden marriage."

"I'll meet with the prosecutor," Charlie said, "and see if we can reach a deal."

"Good idea," I concurred.

Mandy smiled again and said, "Do you think he'll take a deal?"

"Depends," Charlie said, "but it might beat fighting through a trial just to see you acquitted. We'll see. I'll see if he can meet me at lunch."

I looked at my watch. It was 8:35 a.m.

"I'm going to leave Mandy in your hands, Charlie. Maybe I can dig up something."

Charlie nodded, and I stood to leave. Mandy squeezed my hand and said, "Max, thank you for everything. I'm sorry you got this involved."

"You know me. Anything for a friend." I kissed her hand and left the office.

37

I walked out onto the street and into the glaring morning sun. I wanted to talk to Tom, but I figured that he would also be on his way to court.

I considered calling Lisa. She had been a great help, but I was feeling a bit guilty about calling her after last night. Not that I had a reason; I hadn't anchored my ship in any bay in a long time. Nonetheless, I decided to wait until after breakfast.

I crossed Main Street and stepped onto the curb. I wasn't starving, but the thought of a cup of coffee did get my engine running. I was passing a small diner on the corner of Main and Court Street that had a sign in the window that read, "Hot Coffee." There was no sign declaring the name of the diner, just that it had hot coffee. That seemed like the only thing important to me.

I pushed the door open, and a cowbell strapped to the handle jangled loudly causing everyone in the diner to turn toward me.

"Just have a seat," a cute waitress, who I guessed was no more than 22, said, "and I'll be right with you."

I found an empty booth and slid onto the bench. I took a moment to scan the room. There were about eight customers in the whole joint. I was beginning to feel an ease come over me. It may have been the beautiful morning that made one feel good to be alive, or it may be the way things had been snapping into place so quickly. I had a good feeling, and I was certain that Charlie Nichols would have no problem in the trial. Of course, he was right. We needed something more concrete to ensure a victory.

My phone came alive with the sound of

the William Tell Overture, or for the more ignorant, The Lone Ranger Theme.

I answered.

"Hey," Lisa said, "Where are you?"

So much for waiting to call her. "At this little diner across from the courthouse trying to get a cup of coffee."

"Hoffman's?" she asked.

"I don't know. There was no sign. It said hot coffee. I wanted hot coffee. So I came inside."

"Sounds good. Want some company?"

I didn't mind the idea of companionship. Although I think if she'd have asked two days ago, I would have said no. Today I was grateful she had been along.

"Sure," I answered. "Want me to order you a cup?"

"No," she said, "I'll be there in ten minutes. I want it hot."

I hung up with her and laid the phone on the table.

The young waitress approached the

table, and her name tag proclaimed her to be Becky. She smiled a beautiful smile that made her big brown eyes glitter. Her nose wrinkled as she smiled. All I could do was grin at her.

"Would you like a cup of coffee?" she asked me.

"Yes, ma'am."

Becky turned and walked toward the counter. She had long, dark brown hair that stopped between her shoulder blades. I turned away and shook her image from my head.

She returned a minute later with my coffee and a small container of cream. "Would you like a menu?" she asked.

"Yes, please," I said with a smile. I was struck by the notion that while she was no super model, although she was cute, she was one of those people that just exuded joy. I felt good being around her.

She was handing me a menu and saying, "I'll give you a minute," when Lisa walked through the door.

"Hi Becky," Lisa said as she slid into the booth across from me.

"Hey, Lisa," Becky's voice inflated as she greeted Lisa. "So are you joining him?"

"Yes," Lisa replied.

"He's a cutie," Becky said, and I think all the blood rushed to my cheeks.

"It's not like that," Lisa said.

"Now," I interrupted, "let Becky talk."

Both of them laughed. I tried to keep the color in my cheeks from getting too bright. Becky cut the fun when she told Lisa she would bring another menu.

"You cheatin' on me?" Lisa asked.

I looked over my menu. She was smiling.

"I didn't know we were exclusive," I said before I lowered my eyes behind my menu.

"Here you go Lisa." Becky laid a menu on the table in front of Lisa.

"Thanks," Lisa said as Becky turned

away. Then she looked at me,

"Don't worry. Once you get a taste of me, you'll be demanding exclusivity."

I peered over my menu at her again. She was reading her menu, and I was not willing to bet that she was wrong.

Becky returned in time to save me, and I ordered two breakfast chops and some scrambled eggs. Lisa ordered a cup of coffee and a plate of scrambled eggs and sausage.

"What's new?" Lisa asked me after Becky shuffled off to get our breakfast.

"I was talking to Austin Knox last night. We were talking about how Mark's clothes were found."

"How were they found?" she asked.

"I don't know. I meant to ask Charlie Nichols if it was in his file. I am sure he had the police report. But it might be interesting if you were trying to figure what had happened before he was shot. Did he take the time to make them neat, or did he just throw them around?"

"That's a good idea. I can call and see if someone at the station might tell me."

I nodded, "What bothers me is how the whole scene feels staged. The killer might have even stripped him naked to further the speculation. He seemed to plan it out."

"Or she," Lisa added.

I eyed Lisa. "An equal opportunity murder?"

"It just seems that the chances of Mark Lofton taking his clothes off on his own for a man might be slim. Unless we are missing another angle of his life."

"Maybe," I acknowledged, "but he did weigh almost 200 pounds. So unless his killer convinced him to take off his clothes then he or she had to do strip him after he was shot."

"The whole thing is probably moot," Lisa said, "but the killer could be a he or a she."

"Or both. Maybe it's a horse of a completely different color. A shotgun-toting she-male."

Lisa snorted, "We don't get a whole lot of those in these parts."

"It takes all sorts."

Lisa sighed with relief when our food came and our conversation ended.

We both ate quietly. My eggs were pretty runny.

"So do you think the money is really out there somewhere?" Lisa asked between bites.

I finished chewing the driest piece of pork to ever cross my lips. Once I washed the pork down with some eggs, I answered her, "I don't know. I figure that if the money is out there in cash, then the killer probably thought Leigh had it. Otherwise, she knew something that he or she didn't want her talking about."

"Either way we won't ever know," Lisa stated.

"Maybe. Mandy gave me an idea about someplace that Lofton might have hidden it."

"Where?" Lisa said with a mouthful of toast.

"Now that's lady-like."

"Sorry," she murmured past the toast in her mouth.

"Mandy said she couldn't think of anyplace that he could have hidden it in her house, but there is an old shack on the other side of the mountain from Mandy's place. It's about a mile hike, but it might be secluded enough."

"Isn't that Russell Mountain?" She swallowed before asking.

I thought for a minute. I couldn't remember if I ever knew the name of the mountain, and I shook my head. "I don't remember."

"Then if you know the way, I vote we go for another hike."

"Then eat up."

I finished eating my mediocre chops by greasing them down my throat with the water that this diner called eggs. Yet, I could see myself coming back in again if for no other reason than to feel good about myself. As the diner filled with more customers, I imagined I wasn't the only one with that opinion.

I was waiting for Becky to total our bill when my phone began to dance and sing across the table. I reached for it and answered.

"Max," said Austin, "how are you?"

"Just grand."

"I figured if I could hook up with you then I might stand a good chance of being on the front lines when this case gets broken."

I glanced across the table at Lisa. I was beginning to feel like Fred in the Scooby Gang. I decided that it wouldn't hurt. Besides that might be one more head to put together.

"Lisa and I are about to do a little search for the missing money. It's probably a long shot, but you are welcome to join us."

"Where are we looking?"

Becky arrived with our bill which totaled a grand $7.82. I gave her fifteen. She deserved the extra $6.18.

I continued to talk, "Mandy mentioned the old shack. Remember the one back behind her place."

"Oh yeah," Austin replied. "Perfect."

"I suppose we can meet at Mandy's and hike up there."

Austin suggested, "Or we can meet back at your boat. I've got a Jeep; we can drive almost all the way there now."

"Really." We had never been able to drive up there, or at least we never did.

"Yeah," Austin explained, "I think there are some four wheeler trails that have gotten bigger over the years."

"It beats walking. We can meet you in about 20 minutes."

Lisa and I left Hoffman's Diner. The

sun beamed down on us as we made our way back to my car.

38

Austin was waiting for us in the marina parking lot when we arrived. He was lounging in a white Jeep Wrangler that had no top. Mud was splattered up the sides and over the tires showing signs that this Jeep had seen its fair share of off road trails. Austin looked like he was basking in the morning sun.

I locked my car, and Lisa and I walked toward the Jeep. The morning was warming up nicely.

"Hop in," Austin shouted.

"I'll sit in the back," I told Lisa.

"No," she insisted, "you need the leg room."

I wrinkled my brow, but I didn't argue. I gave her my hand to help her climb into the back seat. I grabbed the roll bar and pulled myself into the front seat.

"Let's go find some money," Austin said.

He pulled onto the highway and floored it. The Jeep jumped to the task as the wheels screamed. I glanced back at Lisa who was pulling her hair back so that the wind wouldn't tangle it. Once she had it back, she leaned back and seemed to soak the rays of the sun into her golden skin.

Austin asked, "So, do you think the money is there?"

He pulled my attention from Lisa, and I looked at him. "I doubt it. I don't know. I guess we just make sure. I'm not certain the money even really exists."

"What?" Austin exclaimed. "I thought you said he was embezzling."

"Not that there was no money, but I would bet it's electronic. If it were me I would wire it as far away from me as possible."

Austin just nodded, and I continued, "I just think it's strange that he put it in his own account."

Lisa leaned forward, "I don't think he was a brain surgeon."

"Maybe he put it there so he could wire it. Didn't think anyone would notice."

I shrugged, "Then he certainly was no brain surgeon. I just wish we knew how much we are looking for."

"If we find it, can we keep it?" Austin asked.

"No, I'm afraid not."

Lisa tapped Austin on the shoulder and said, "He only says that because he's rich."

"Hey," I argued jokingly, "it's not easy being rich."

"Right," said Austin, "it's a cinch being poor."

"You aren't poor."

"Yeah," Austin said.

The conversation lagged for the next few minutes until we reached the dirt road that leads to Mandy's house. Austin drove past it.

"Where are we going?" I asked.

"I know where some trails are that lead up to the top of the mountain."

I heard Lisa saying, "It is on Russell Mountain."

"Yeah," Austin said.

"Is it close to the boat in the tree?" Lisa asked.

"We have to hike about ten minutes from the boat," Austin explained.

"Boat in the tree?" I asked.

Lisa nodded, "About four years ago, there was a big tornado. Tore the county to bits. Anyway, this guy had his boat carried off. Tornado dropped it seven miles from where it was. Stuck it in this big oak tree about thirty feet off the ground. Everyone decided it would cost too much to salvage and get it down, so it just got left there."

Austin turned down a little dirt road. We had driven almost two miles when the road ended, and a trail lead off the road. Austin slowed and shifted down a few gears before climbing onto the trail. The Jeep bounced along the trail as it ascended the mountain. Rain had washed out some ruts and turned them into ditches. We jolted and jarred across them. The trail curved and wound through the trees as it continued to lead us up the mountain.

Austin slowed the Jeep to a crawl. I looked to my right to see an older bass boat hanging in a tall tree. I shook my head in amazement.

Austin stopped the Jeep on the side of the trail.

"We hike from here," he said.

"I never came this way," I commented.

"This trail wasn't that big when we were kids."

Lisa laughed, "That was big."

Austin got out on his side, and I slid down to the ground. Austin leaned his seat forward to let Lisa out. She climbed out with her hand on the roll bar. Her feet hit the ground, and she stopped.

She looked up at Austin. "Do you smoke?"

"Sometimes," he answered.

She lifted an empty pack of cigarettes that read, "Dunhill." My eyes widened. I glared at Austin for a second. It was one second too long.

The next second whirled past as Austin saw my face. He grabbed Lisa by the hair and slammed her head into the roll bar. I started around the Jeep as Lisa fell to the ground in a heap. Austin jerked his hand up, and the crack of the gun rang through the woods.

I hit the ground. My hands pushed me up as soon as I landed. I dove across the trail and into the woods as a second shot echoed through the trees.

We were near the top of the mountain, and the forest floor was littered with boulders jutting from the earth. I scrambled down the slope and found cover behind a giant stone. My head stung. I touched it to find a bloody mess where a bullet must have grazed me. I wished for my gun. It was still lying on the table in the boat.

Austin was coming, and I had to move quickly. I dashed through the trees and down the mountain. I found another boulder to hide me.

"Max!" he yelled. He was only fifty yards away, which was close enough for him to hit me.

"Come on, Max. There's no place to run."

He was right. If I ran for more cover, then he would eventually be able to hit me. If I waited, then he would simply walk around and shoot me.

"Okay Austin," I yelled. I was trying to think of something.
"Come on out."

I felt a line of blood dripping down my cheek. "Why, Austin?"

"Don't be stupid, Max." It was all he said.

He was taking his time getting to me. Then it occurred to me that he might have thought I had a gun. It didn't matter because I didn't. Once he killed me, he would have to finish Lisa. I hoped she was okay and maybe able to run.

I looked around for better cover. My foot kicked something hard, and I looked down at a beat up boat propeller. I looked up to see the bass boat hanging from a tree only twenty feet away.

"Alright Max, it's over."

He was just the other side of the boulder. I grabbed the propeller. I moved quickly to the side of the boulder. I jumped out and tried to frisbee the propeller at Austin. My plan failed quickly as the prop wasn't as aerodynamic as I had hoped. It spiraled down and struck him in his leg. The prop ripped his pants. It didn't slow him down.

"Sorry Max," he said finally.

"Me too," I said as I stared down the barrel of a .38 that looked to me like a cannon. I wanted to close my eyes.

The third shot was immediately followed by a fourth. I hit the ground before I heard either of them. I could see the clouds in the sky above the trees.

"Max!" I heard Lisa cry. Then I saw her kneeling beside me. She lifted me up. My shoulder burned. Austin was lying on the ground. His eyes stared at me without moving.

Lisa was talking but I couldn't make sense of anything yet. Everything happened too fast for me to comprehend yet. She had blood all over her face. I looked on the ground next to her. A small .22 was lying there.

"...got a shot off. Sorry." she was saying as she unbuttoned my shirt. I looked at the front of my shirt the black fabric was dark and wet.

Lisa ripped the shirt away from my shoulder. There was a hole the size of a quarter with a stream of dark blood flowing from it.

"We need to get you to the hospital. I think you will be okay."

"Ow," I moaned, "I've never been shot before."

She helped me to my feet.

"Where'd you get the gun?" I asked.

"I was raised by Sammy Day. I always carry it in my bag. I'm not a bad shot."

I glanced back at Austin's body and said, "I guess not."

"I was pissed."

"I'm glad," I said. Then I added, "We need his keys."

Lisa stepped over to his body and fished his keys out of his pocket. I felt the forest begin to sway. I leaned against the boulder. Lisa put her arm around me to help me up the hill.

39

Lisa called Scott Gaither once we started back down the mountain. She gave him the details, and he said he would send a squad car to escort us to the hospital.

There were two squad cars coming on the highway as we turned off the dirt road. One did a u-turn, and the deputy driving signaled for us to follow him. The other was heading to the crime scene.

My shoulder was burning and numb at the same time. I thanked God when we hit the asphalt. My arm couldn't take the bumps much more. The adrenaline rush had subsided and the pain was beginning.

was waiting for us at the hospital.

room where a Dr. James

and proceeded to

extract a .38 slug from my shoulder. It only took 25 minutes to clean me up and bandage my shoulder. He cleaned the gash on my head and put a small bandage on it.

Scott had taken Lisa to another room to have her treated as well. She gave him her statement while receiving 15 stitches in her forehead. He came for my statement when he had finished talking to her.

"Feeling alright?" he asked.

"Yeah, just great."

He retorted, "I told you not to get involved."

"Don't gloat. I learned my lesson."

It was almost 11:30 a.m. This had been a long morning. I stood up, and my legs wobbled a bit. Scott steadied me.

"You might want to sit," he suggested.

"No, I need a ride."

Scott was reluctant, but he was fairly easy to convince when I explained to him what I needed to do. He and I left the hospital in his squad car.

The courthouse was only three miles from the hospital. Scott pulled into his own parking spot in front of the courthouse.

It was almost lunch. The court employees were filled with the anticipation of it. Scott led me to a small room that was used for conferences. He then delivered my message to Tom.

At ten minutes past noon, the door opened. Tom and Charlie Nichols entered first. They were immediately followed by Mandy.

"Max!" she said, "What are...What happened?"

"Austin's dead."

"What?" She stepped back.

"Yeah, it seems he killed Leigh Rosen."

"Oh my god," she exclaimed, "Did he ʿark?"

ʾu did."

me silently.

 long had you and

She held her stare on me as she said, "We weren't. We were just friends."

"Sorry, Austin kind of confessed to me," I lied. "Actually he was bragging. It was stupid. The kind of thing that people do in movies.

"But he did think he was going to kill me. I guess you guys were wrong about that."

She didn't speak.

"It was a beautiful trap. I walked right into it. I just have too many lives."

Charlie Nichols and Tom had been sitting there just as stunned as Mandy. Charlie suddenly regained his senses. "Mr. Sawyer, this is uncalled for. I must object."

"Go ahead and object. This isn't official yet. By the way, Charlie, I won't be paying the bill after all. It's nothing personal with you. I just don't appreciate being tricked, not to mention being shot.

"I believe Tom may be willing to accept a change of plea."

Mandy studied me and asked, "Did you kill him?"

"No, I had no idea. Lisa Day figured out he killed Leigh Rosen before he could shoot us in the back. Thankfully, Mr. Day taught his little girl not to trust anyone. I wish someone had taught me that."

I stood up. I was still shaky, but I didn't want to show it.

"I never asked for your help," Mandy declared.

"I know. In fact, you might have gotten away with it if I hadn't come. I was certain that you were innocent."

I thought I could see her eyes beginning to tear up. I turned toward the door. I put my hand on the knob. With my back facing her, ˉ said stonily, "Confess Mandy. Tell them ͻle story, or I will take the stand. I ˋ do that."

ᵈoor and walked out of the ᶜlosed. I walked ˎ down on a wooden bench. I sat and stared at the wall for nearly twenty minutes before Tom sat beside me.

"You okay?"

"No," I answered.

"She's giving a confession right now."

"I knew she would."

Tom cleared his throat, "She asked me to tell you that she was sorry."

"Remember the other day, when I said I would find out who the killer was?

"Yes, I knew you would."

"I wish I hadn't."

Tom didn't say a thing. He put his arm around me.

40

Three days passed since Mandy made her confession. I had only seen Lisa for a few moments on Monday afternoon. She had been at her computer for two days putting the story together.

The Barnes County News had beaten the Arkansas Ledger to the punch. Lisa worked overtime to get her paper out early. The Little Rock paper did reprint her story. The story seemed to come straight from a soap opera.

Mandy and Austin had been having an a while. They hatched a half-

Austin had been involved with d used her connection at nearly two million t by marrying

Mark, he could become their patsy.

Mandy had, likewise, situated Mark into the strip club and his sudden marriage. The truth was that Mark was deeply in love with Mandy. He had told her about Leigh Rosen. When Mandy told him to marry her to take advantage of her, he blindly agreed. He thought the marriage to Leigh Rosen would be short lived. It was, but so was he.

The money had been moved around until it landed in an off-shore account. Mandy had used Mark's accounts so that the paper trail would stay with him. My arrival was the only wrench in their plans.

"Here's what I don't understand," Lisa said as we sat beneath the stars on the deck of the boat, "Why bother killing us? We were helping to prove she didn't do it."

"Steve Reynolds," I answered. "The Little Rock PD found him Monday morning while we were getting closer to nature. He had been shot in the head with a .38. We were only a phone call away from connecting everything. Austin had to make a clean sweep."

Lisa took a sip of wine, "He would have killed us easily."

I agreed as I poured another glass of the 1998 Cakebread Cabernet Sauvignon. "He would have gotten us in the back of the head when we weren't looking. Then he would have probably hidden our bodies in the woods where we wouldn't be found for a long time. I suppose it wasn't the smartest thing we have ever done, letting him drive us deep into the woods. It's a good thing you solved it so quickly."

"Yay for me," she said gleefully. Then she asked, "But how did you figure out that ᵕdy was involved too?"

ʰile the doctor was taking the slug ᵗarted thinking about the ᵇ-male. Then it occurred to ʰeen both male and ⁿut it being a she."

"Besides Mandy had used Austin as her alibi. He should have never been connected. We hadn't even considered him."

Lisa took another drink. "Scott said that the Cells Etc. guy picked out his photo, and they found the cell phone he had used."

"He was cleaning up. Even killed Paul Grace just to get his heat off." I sat back and contemplated. "Still it was pretty smart to frame yourself. I knew it felt too staged."

"I guess it wasn't smart enough. Though we just got lucky."

I shook my head, "No, we would have figured out something when Steve Reynolds turned up dead."

"No," Lisa reminded me, "we would have been found dead in the woods with .38 slugs in our heads."

She was right. I tried to put the glass down, and my shoulder felt like someone had stuck me with a knife. I winced

"Are you okay?" Lisa asked as she moved over next to me and took my glass.

feel bad that you got shot. It was my fault. I guess I owe you one."

"Not really," I said, "after all if it weren't for you, he probably would have gotten me in the head."

"Then I guess you owe me." She leaned toward me.

Our lips touched, and we kissed for an eternity that didn't seem to last long enough. She pulled back and looked at me. I had the biggest grin on my face.

"What is it?" she asked.

"You are right again."

"About what?"

"I want exclusivity," I demanded.

"Yay for me."

Want more of Max? Read his other adventures

Blood Remembered

Baptism of Blood

Blood Stained

Bloody History

Crimson Blood

Blood River

Want a free story? Visit

www.douglas-pratt.com

Made in the USA
Middletown, DE
03 January 2025